THE LAND OF ICK AND ECK

Harlot's Encounters

VOLUMES ONE, TWO, THREE

Also by Micah Genest

Three Stories About Children Who Die

The Beginning

Micah Genest

The Land of Ick and Eck
Harlot's Encounters

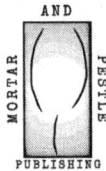

AND
MORTAR PESTLE
PUBLISHING

First Printing 2018

Printed Somewhere

Copyright © 2018 Micah Genest

All Rights Reserved

Illustrations by John Bauer obtained through the public domain.

For permission rights, contact the publisher at the address below:

mortarandpestlepublishing.com
info@mortarandpestlepublishing.com

Caution: This is a work of fiction. Though names, characters, incidents, situations, or other may sound familiar, they are products of the author's imagination, simply used in a fictitious manner. Any resemblance to actual persons, or realities, which there definitely are, either that be of persons living or dead, or perhaps of passed or of future events, they are to be understood as purely "coincidental," for that is the life we have agreed on, is it not? Thus, it is to be said, these are a simple parade of unforeseen happenings in which we agree to never have seen.

Mortar and Pestle Publishing
ISBN 978-1-7753721-4-1

THIS PAGE
(AND THE NEXT AND THE NEXT)
OUTLINE THE CONTENTS OF THIS BOOK

VOLUME I

VOLUME II

CHAPTER

VOLUME III

CHAPTER

THE END

this book is dedicated to the forgotten children
and her

** The following presented is the first, second, and third
volumes of Harlot's encounters in the Land of Ick and Eck **

Into a land of fantasy
With haste we cast them all aside
No tearing if you cannot see
That is what we all make-believe

Volume I

CHAPTER I

HARLOT IN A FIELD

Over the mountains and by a tree, there was a girl, and her name was Harlot. She was a comely fair size headed person who enjoyed wearing a blue rose tangled in her hair, as well as a dress upon her body. At times, Harlot was known to get a little disagreeable (but we all do one time or another, so let us not judge her too harshly). Also, the girl seemed to always be looking at things, different things, leaping from one sight to another. Likewise, she had the tendency of quickly forgetting things too, so she was quite the adventurous sort as well. And lastly, on a quite serious note, Harlot was lacking in discernment: she possessed an innocent and a much too trusting character, which inhibited her, like most, to truly see a rotten plum from a pleasant one.

Now, there were two boys, who happened to be brothers, and they had the tendency of bothering every being they could find, especially Harlot, as she was so often absent minded; she fell into their mischievous traps time and time again.

So on a day, when the girl found herself before the two boys, little did she expect what was to be ahead of her.

"Hello Charles. Hello Alexander. I seem unable to find my drinking cup; I think a bone-grubber took it by mistake.

In any case, I was wondering if one of you would let me borrow one of yours for a moment so I could put some water in it," asked Harlot to the two boys, for Charles and Alexander were their names.

"How dare you call me Charles...Harlot...Tartlet," retorted one of the boys who had a visible temper. "Ha, that is quite funny, Harlot...Tartlet. I believe that is what I shall call you from now on. Harlot Tartlet...bullocks, I have forgotten my train of thought."

"You dimwitted brother," lectured the other boy with a supposed intelligence, for he was the older of the two. "Always trailing off onto wherever your soft head takes you. It is quite a silly name I would have to agree, but I do believe you mentioned something about your own name before you went prattling on about how clever you were for coming up with Tartlet Harlot."

"You are the dimwitted one, Alex. It is Harlot Tartlet, not Tartlet Harlot," corrected Charles in an irritated manner.

"I do not really care what you are going on about Chuck," mocked the older brother. "I have the slightest interest in continuing this topic any further."

By this time, Harlot was showing her teeth in a grand smile, for she was quite pleased that the argument was about her; though, the girl would have preferred it to be about how pretty her blue rose was, or other marvelous things like that.

"Oh well," whispered Harlot to herself.

"Aha, now I remember," rallied Charles. "My name is Chuck, not Charles. How many times must I tell you this...Harlot Tartlet?"

The girl looked sternly at the boy, and then announced with pride and passion, and a dash or two of some other things, "Always a few more…Charles."

Immediately, Harlot fell to the ground laughing, for this seemed to amuse her.

When finished, she stood back up and spoke with much seriousness, "I really am thirsty though."

It was then that Alexander came up with a brilliant idea, so he thought; he knew his brother would dearly appreciate the outcome.

"Of course we shall fetch you some water," planned Alexander, with mischievous intentions. "It would be our pleasure."

"Have you gone mad brother," responded Charles, unaware of Alexander's intentions. "I will not do her biddings."

"Be quite," hissed the older brother, quietly but harshly. "Just do as I say."

So then the two brothers went off to fetch the girl something to drink, and the child quietly sat on a nearby rock, underneath a tree, and waited.

Much time passed before she saw the two boys heading back.

"Hello Harlot," greeted Charles in an amused manner, not adding in the later ingenious addition he had previously come up with.

"We have brought a cup with water for you," cunningly announced the other brother in a courtly fashion.

Since Harlot was a civilized person, she did not gulp the liquid down all at once, though she desperately wanted to; instead, she sipped it with her little finger dangling in the air.

As the girl did this, the younger of the two brothers fell to the ground laughing. Alexander looked at Charles with much annoyance, but then he too could not help himself and so fell to the ground in a similar fashion. The two boys laughed and laughed, even after their sides began to feel as if the bones in their chests would burst out from within at any moment.

Yet, the girl did not pay any attention to them, for she was very thirsty, and the water felt so nice as it made its way down her throat. But as the perching liquid began to reduce in its amount, she noticed that there was something strange at the bottom of the cup; nevertheless, she kept on taking civil sips. This continued until Harlot clearly saw what the curious thing was; when revelation came, she screamed, and then dropped both cup and tears.

A mouse was at the bottom.

"You...you...you..." stuttered the tricked girl.

It was not clear if those were the words that came from the child's mouth, for it was quite difficult to understand them through the deafening screaming and crying, as well as the two boys' laughing.

When things seemed to settle down for a moment, Harlot assured, "I will get you for this, you...you queer plungers. Revenge will be upon you, the both of you."

The girl ran as fast as her little legs could take her to the place she kept warm at night, where she continued to cry. Tears would have dripped from her eyes for hours if it were not for one of her sisters, who asked what was the matter. Harlot did not reply through words, for all she did was inwardly contrive plans of vengeance, while making incomprehensible noises. Once she grew tired of this for the time being, the girl sat up, went and washed herself with the other girls, made dinner, and then ate the leftovers.

Harlot went to bed quietly that night, but her mind was the very opposite. She had a head of redress, but did not know where to begin.

In the end, the girl decided that she would further explore her options in the morning.

So she then fell asleep.

CHAPTER II

A PLACE

When the child awoke, she immediately decided to collect some faggots. For the reason that there were too few sticks to be found in the first place she looked, Harlot decided to search in a nearby woodland, and so brought her body to the front of a great bunch of trees, then walked frontwards, aiming for a centre place; her mind had the impression that the very best sticks would be the furthest in. The girl walked and walked, and then tripped, owing to her clumsy person, then got up and walked some more. In due time, she grew tired of walking and so sat down on a log.

"Mary. Marie. Mayree," called an anxious voice in a whisper.

"How very odd. My name is not Mary, Marie, or Mayree," contemplated Harlot.

Naturally, her mind was suddenly consumed by the sight of a bunch of sticks sticking out from the edges of a muddy game trail.

"Oh my, a maze. A very long maze at that. It must go on for a very long time if it is that muddy. But if only it were possible to know where it goes," went on the wondering girl.

Harlot took a few more moments, dedicating them completely to thought. But then, when she had become ready to lose her head because of the possibilities, a small snigger came from behind a nearby tree.

"Who is there? Come out so that I may see your face," demanded the girl.

"Never never. No. I can't. I won't. I shonte," wheezed the voice in a disturbing squeaky tone.

"You shonte? Is that even proper English?" corrected Harlot, finding herself clever for pointing out the error the voice had made.

A moment passed in which seemed to be too long for the girl to wait, so she walked towards the tree that she believed the voice to be coming from; the child was not frightened of strangers, for she was an innocent little girl.

"Where are you?" chuckled Harlot, enjoying the game at hand.

Suddenly, the voice behind the tree broke out in an attack, "Listen here you wee thing. You shall do as I say."

"Aha! I believe I have found you. I knew it! I knew it from the start. You are behind the tree…are you not?" exclaimed and then questioned the girl, ignoring the words and tone of the voice.

And slowly, out from behind the bend of the tree came a small creature much shorter than she: His face was wrinkled and his teeth were clean; he wore a cotton red hat on his head and black iron boots on his feet; the nails on his unpleasant fingers where skinny and crooked; and the loose fabric on his chest smelt freshly tanned. Harlot thought the thing looked quite silly with his long brown robe that went down to his ankles; she could tolerate the colour brown, so she did not mind his presence much.

"No time for this my dear," squeaked the figure, politically changing into a politer tone. "You need to come quick, for I have something delightful to show you. You do like delightful things don't you?"

"Why of course I do silly. I like all kinds of things for that matter. I like green things, yellow things, big things and small things. I like when things are blue especially. That is my favorite colour you know," told the child.

"Come now please," gallantly requested the small creature. "Just follow me. Right this way."

Harlot did not make it a general rule to follow strangers about when she was not forced to, but she found the little man's hat interesting to look at, so red as it was, so she went where he went.

It was not long before they stopped in front of a tree covered in a fabric similar to that on the thing's chest. The small man moved aside some of the coverings to expose a hole, which he pulled at. The girl laughed, for the scene looked quite queer as the figure struggled to do something to the tree, but she was very interested. Eventually, the time came and Harlot was coaxed into entering inside, and then they crawled up, then down, then up, then down again, and then up once more.

"How very strange this tree is. It looked much smaller on the outside, and it looked as if it went straight up like all the others. But this one goes up, then down, then up, then down again, and then up once more," educated Harlot aloud, while the small creature took no notice of what she said.

All the while, the girl pressed her imagination forwards with ideas that she was to soon be met with fields of pink daisies and purple goat lilies, all enclosed by rose bushes of every colour and every kind imaginable. She did not know why she had such high expectations; she just thought it was to be so. Yet, after they finally reached a small, empty, round room, climbed a little ladder, opened a little round door upon the ceiling, and then crawled out, all Harlot saw were several dirt paths surrounded by a dense woodland. Each path looked as dreadful as the next, and ugly, very ugly.

"Come along my dear," insisted the stranger. "I must show you something. Quick!"

And so they went along a path, which the man knew very well.

"How unsightly. There is not one flower no matter where I look," murmured the girl.

When the travel became long and tiresome for the child, she picked up a few pebbles from off the ground and threw them at the man, hoping he would entertain her in some manner; he did not seem to mind in the least, for his mind was pressed upon the hopes of other things.

The stranger did eventually say, "Stray along into the home my dear," when they arrived in front of a ruin resembling an old peel tower; once inside, he politely spoke again. "Let us get you seated my dear."

The thing called upon another similar looking thing like him, except that her brown dress dropped down even closer to the ground. The amount of brown was much less tolerable to Harlot; there was much too much of it.

"Oh," hushed the wicked-woman-creature.

The wicked-man-creature smiled.

(In orthodox expurgated detail:)

It was at this time that the wicked-man-creature took the child's blue rose, blew on it, and then ate it; the wicked-woman-creature paid no deniable attention. While Harlot did not understand what had happened, she would have certainly cut off her nose beforehand if she had been cloistered.

When finished, an awfully long silence followed until the girl broke out in tears and stomped on the ground.

"Oh whatever is the matter," asked the wicked-man-creature in a remorseless voice.

"This house is ugly and I would very much care for some food to fill my stomach. You made me walk that entire unsightly path and now you do not even offer me a comfortable place to place myself," protested Harlot, trying to forget about her blue rose, confused and ignorant.

"Oh forgive me my quean," mocked the wicked-man-creature.

To no surprise, the girl was very much pleased by the wicked-man-creature's vocabulary, a queen she thought, as she did not perceive the way he spoke; it also made her think of something other than the present situation.

"Let me get you onto something warm so you may be comfortable," scoffed the wicked-man-creature, while romping in circles, reveling at his feat.

Thus, Harlot was placed onto a metal sheet above a fire lined with something wet.

With much irritation to the pair, the girl cried out in anger, "What do you think you are doing? Now I am all wet and have no dry cloths to change into and it looks as if the sun is about to set so I cannot dry them and will now have no dry clothes to sleep in."

"We'll figure something out," retorted the annoyed wicked-man-creature, as he smeared a bit of something grainy onto Harlot's back.

As time passed, the wetness on the sheet became warmer and warmer, and then hotter and hotter; the girl grew quite heated. She wanted to say something, but she felt too sleepy and began to doze off. This went on until the little couple began to feel impatient, so they put a tin dome over her head, consequently trapping her inside a very dark and very hot chamber.

This woke Harlot up.

She could hear many voices and sounds from all directions, but they were all muffled, as if she was in another room.

"Let me out this instant! It is too hot to stay in here and it is too dark to see," screamed the girl at the top of her lungs.

Suddenly, the metal covering was lifted over Harlot's head and then crashed onto the ground with a loud DaDang! The girl fell onto the floor, while the dome dropped on top of the newly scalding couple.

"What an event," thought Harlot to herself.

Now placed in front of her was a fat-Friar. The fellow spoke several words in the direction of the wicked-creatures and then took the girl's arm and pulled her out of the situation; she could see the couple trying to get up when at a far distance, but in the end they did not.

CHAPTER III

A MEETING WITH A FAT-FRIAR

"Delight me and follow," insisted the droll looking fellow. "We shall leave this place at once."

They were now standing upon another dirt path.

"But I am all wet. I must dry myself off first. Then we may go, whenever I decide," told Harlot with frustration, for she did not like the wetness upon her.

"No," replied the stranger.

"Whatever are you talking about, you, you—" shouted the girl, which turned into a stutter.

"Silence yourself," interrupted the fat-Friar in a tempered manner. "Follow me and quit the wandering of that useless tongue."

Harlot ran a distance with the stranger at a reasonably quick pace for a girl with short legs, watching the thinning trees, until they eventually came to a set new of passageways.

"Come along now, this way," instructed the fellow, after selecting another trail.

It was then that Harlot noticed along the edges of this dirt path laboured worker bees that buzzed and buzzed as they did their business very busily. She could see, but did not understand why, each of them carried cheesecloths full of honey with wild thyme sticking out; when a bag happened to be full, the bee would drop it into a bucket of hot water, which created an invigorating scent.

"What a waste. I protest!" declared the girl aloud.

Inevitably, fettered by the spectacle, she misplaced one of her feet and sprawled out onto the ground; every bee stopped what it was doing at once and began to laugh at Harlot, who now laid helplessly in the middle of the crowd of crude spectators.

And then all the bees broke into song:

Fancy a drop of porridge
Or perhaps a tin-bucked shoe
Drop a morsel of your bread
Into a pint of glue
Sing ya ee ya ee ya ee
Ya ee ya ee ya
Ya ee ya ee ya ee ya ee
Ya ee ya ee ya
Ee ya

There was more to the song, but the fat-Friar was very impatient and so pulled the girl into a certain direction, and continued on the path until they reached a folly, which they quickly entered.

"It would give me pleasure if you were to place yourself on the floor, my little laundress," told the stranger, as he offered Harlot a bowl of soup; however, the girl unknowingly rejected the binding invitation by singing to herself a little too loudly.

"I have to say," began the fat-Friar, expecting to give a long speech, "I am a humble fellow indeed, so very humble. Oh yes I am—"

Yet, to the stranger's dismay, Harlot broke the sermon and asked a question, for she began to grow bored of the subject, "I do believe you never told me your name. What do I call you?"

"My name is of no business of yours," asserted the fellow conceitedly.

"This cannot be true!" declared the girl with much hostility.

No words were spoken for some time between the two. Then Harlot thought of another question.

But before she could say what was now in her mind, the stranger announced, "The length of your useless holiday is over. If you stay any longer, I expect coin or some lipping arguments. And which do I prefer at the moment? Come on girl, do not waste my time."

Once again, there was silence, just like a moment ago. However, Harlot still had a strong desire to ask the question that continued to play within her mind. It was not a very polite question, but in the end she did not take concern of its offense: "What is it that you are?"

"I am a man of course!" retorted the fat-Friar in anger, joined with the fact that there was to be no immediate gain to the visit. "What else would I be you stupid girl."

And with those last words, and with much to think about, Harlot ran off and out of the place by herself.

CHAPTER IV

UP IN A TREE

The girl soon found herself upon a path brimmed with trees on every side, even in the middle. She imagined that such a sight could only be possible if every tree had little feet under their trunks, each holding onto the dirt so tightly they could drink the rainwater that seeped down towards them, as if they were made of sponge cakes, fighting for each and every last drop. That could be the only explanation. Some trees were yellow, while others where yellow too, and others were green, purple, or red, and sometimes and. When sunlight struck onto their leaves, or branches, they grew into other different colours, while others grew different altogether. Some did not even look like trees anymore.

In due time, Harlot made her way into a small village. Since there was no more tugging from here to there, she took notice of her surroundings, like how there were awkwardly shaped buildings spaced ever so close together, some made of many windows, while others had hardly any at all, if any, for that was an expensive luxury, though most were shattered, as it had been the Night of Broken Glass but the week before. The scattered chimneys about, which pushed their way out from both the top and bottom of buildings, all puffed strings of black sailing smoke, like mile high candy ropes from the heavens. About the streets were petty chimney sweepers that sounded out their daily squalls. By the corner of a gewgaw shop was a panhandler who spoke its salient mind. Besides this, there was much else that was usually forgotten, even the eyes of a youthful damsel that met with Harlot's from behind a window somewhere. The girls looked on with a blurring innocence.

Yet, when a cry began to jingle in the air, and having a curious person, Harlot went to see where it was coming from. The girl inspected all around the place she thought the voice was coming from, but it was nowhere to be seen.

Then the sound sounded twice more: "I am stuck in a place. I need assistance."

"In what place are you stuck?" questioned Harlot audibly.

"Up here, in a tree," sounded the sound. "I would very much appreciate some assistance."

The girl looked up towards the sound and saw a tree; its leaves and bark were all white, except for a few scattered red fruit. Indeed it was a nice tree to look at, and the fruit looked nice as well, quite delicious. How she enjoyed the searching, making sure to look at every branch, and behind almost every leaf. But alas, as all games eventually come to an end, the time came when her eyes spotted where the voice was coming from: at the very top of the tree sat an old-man and another living thing.

"What are you doing up there? You look so small so high up; I could squish you with my fingers," teased Harlot, chuckling as she pressed her fingers together in squishing motions before her eyes.

"It was to no fault of my own," told the living thing in a stumpy voice.

"Yes it was," replied the old-man without hesitation.

"No it was not," argued the other.

"Your beliefs fool you," corrected the old-man.

It seemed that listening to the two would be a long and arduous task, so the girl ignored them and did not bother herself to ask them any more questions. To keep herself occupied, she looked around for something to aid the stranded towards the ground; sooner than later, she found a bundle of rope laying a few feet away. Yet, when Harlot looked up above her head to toss it, sunlight struck the occupied tree and made it look like a different tree altogether. She waited until the sun moved away to be certain that this was indeed the right tree; it was. The girl then placed the rope next to the old man and the other, who made their way to the safety of the ground, no longer at risk to be stuck in the tree for the rest of their lives.

(I will now take the time to describe the two in little detail.)

The old-man was quite tall compared to Harlot, even though he lost half his height from crouching ever so close to the ground. It was not only age that gave him an arched back, but also the habit of picking up forgotten coins from off the ground. To help, but it did nothing in the least, he carried a very straight and short cane.

The other living thing was a little more than half the tallness of Harlot, and was the type that stood on all four feet. He looked similar in age to the old-man, but moved a little more swiftly. Also, he resembled a tortoise. (I suppose we shall call him a tortoise then, since we do not know any better.)

Many thanks were passed round and round until hands and mouths grew tired and no more could be passed.

"Tell me now! What were you both doing up that tree in the first place," questioned the heroic girl, feeling quite excited.

"Well," began the old-man, "my acquaintance wanted to climb that tree for no particular reason. That is, except for the hidden intention of getting us both stuck."

"You are quite the deceitful and insatiate old man," rebutted the tortoise. "It was you who wanted to go up the tree to catch a Butter-Maiden. I specifically remember you saying that you wanted one that resembled a quean of Ick."

"A pocket full of freshness, if I may say," gushed the old-man. "Just like you my dear girl, but not quite."

Harlot blushed, but then a question arose to her mind.

"What is a Butter-Maiden?" asked the girl politely, which was rather unusual or usual, or perhaps both; this might have been due to the fact that she had begun to grow quite fond of the pair.

"Why, it is the most beautiful and wonderful thing you could ever press your seeing eyes on and your blind eye through," replied the old-man, with a stiffening excitement. "Some are white and others are not, but most have fresh hair only on their heads. They have the most adorable eyes, green eyes actually, just like yours little girl. They are difficult to catch in some places, but that is one reason why they are so desirable. But only one. Oh yes. Yes! I get quite excited just imagining them. They hold the most beautiful blue on the edge of the flowers they hold about themselves.

I think they look like baby cats, but not quite. Also, they are made almost entirely of something like warm soft butter, which is possibly the reason they are so difficult to catch, for they will slip right out of your fingers as if your own hands where made of butter as well."

"How delightful! How evocative!" exclaimed Harlot rather loudly, becoming reasonably roused herself.

"Oh yes very delightful indeed," assured the old-man. "I tell you, if a day should pass and you are snatched as one, you will surly become a quean yourself. Yes I say. Those around you will admire you and desires will follow."

"A queen! I would very much like to be a queen!" squealed the girl to herself, thankfully.

How wonderful Harlot thought it would be to be a queen, though she did not really know what royalty meant, except for that their brains are bigger and the such. She imagined, if she were queen, she would be able to have baskets and blankets filled with peaches and blankets, and other nice things like that.

While the girl thought to herself, the tortoise pulled out a piece of white candy, which was made from the red fruit of the white tree he had been trapped in earlier, and put it into his mouth and gave another to the old-man. Harlot became very much interested, for she enjoyed sweet tasting things when place upon her tongue.

"May you give me a piece of candy," politely requested the girl, knowing well that such speech can sometimes get you what you want.

But it was of no use, for the tortoise did not mind her wanting in the least; instead, he became very much interested at the thought of eating Lady's Slippers laced with

Skullcaps, which are some of his favorite types of flowers to nibble on. Thus, they all went wandering about in order to satisfy the tortoise's indulgences, and to keep the old-man's mind on other things.

CHAPTER V

UNDER THE GREEN MOON

When night came, everything that could be seen became the colour of green; it was the fault of the green moon of course, which is known as the Mad Man's Moon. On such a night, most should be weary, for all large and little women, and I suppose their opposites, though not the large, wear the colour of green.

It was at this time that Harlot, the old-man, and the tortoise became spectators to an event consisting of three beings all wearing green waistcoats.

What happened is described below:

Three women standing around a cucking stool:

WOMAN ONE: Shall they clap us in bolts?
WOMAN TWO: Or give us the jolts?
WOMAN THREE: Perhaps they'll glower and cackle our holts.

The three women hide the stool behind a bush and then resume their prior positions.

WOMAN ONE: 'Ohhh!' their little odious pestles cry, 'All are marked as merry delight.' How they pray an un-tasted is their mortar this night.

WOMAN TWO: Of all moons, this one acquits! Gives reason to take what they praise grace gave them to behave. And after, when finished, and safe and sounds all broken by hedges, they toss them aside like dirty mats.

"What are you speaking about?" interrupted the girl.

The three women turn to Harlot with worried expressions.

WOMAN THREE: We must sow our plackets up tight, very tight tonight. Move yourself beyond this place. Get away. We are green. We must get away!

WOMAN ONE: Find some hay!

WOMAN TWO: Find some and stay!

WOMAN THREE: Get away get away!

ALL WOMEN: Get away! Get away!

Exeunt three women.

Once the women were gone, the girl hid in some hay before anyone could see where she went. Eventually, she fell asleep.

CHAPTER VI

THE FISH OF ECK

After Harlot awoke and made herself to the side of the old-man and the tortoise, she was very much surprised to see that an army of armoured fish surrounded her and the others on every side.

"It looks as if there is more iron than anything else," quietly informed the girl to herself.

As well as much iron, each fish held a spear in one fin, balanced a water lily on the other, and sat on a tiny pig covered in a blanket made of wheat and mud, each and all of varying sizes. On a few of the water lilies blossomed grimness in white flowers, which displayed the rank and age of the fish, beginning with the captain down to lower ranks, though none on the youngling soldiers'.

"We are The Fish of Eck," hastily announced the captain, while puffing his gills and pushing out his chest. (You see, he was the largest fish, had the largest spear, largest water lily, largest flower, and sat on the largest tiny pig.) The fish then continued, "Why do you step where you step now?"

"What are you talking about?" whispered Harlot to herself again.

The captain took notice of the girl and her speaking, which he called an outburst, and then demanded, "Who are you girl? And why do you speak?"

"Who are you?" retaliated Harlot in a mimicking scornful tone, loud enough for all to hear.

"Who am I? Ha! I am captain of The Fish of Eck," the captain explained. "I am very important."

The girl was about to add another question to the enquiry session, but she was inhibited to do so.

"Enough with your questions," commanded the largest fish. "There is no time for this wasting. A quean of Eck has lost some of her wardrobe and I am here to search them out."

And with such things said, all of The Fish of Eck began to cheer for the certain quean of Eck, each for their own reasons.

After the fish calmed down to a lower degree of loudness, the captain noticed something in the old-man's hand, "What is it that you have hanging there?"

"These..." nervously began the old-man, "oh yes, these are Lady Slippers. I picked a pair for myself for later, but you can have them, if...if you want."

"I do not need your permission," informed the fish, pushing out his chest even further. "Give them to me now!"

So the old-man did, and the Lady Slippers were a match, being the same size as one another.

"And why do you have these?" demanded the largest fish, trying to hide his excitement. "Where did you get them from?"

"He stole them," shouted one of the armored fish, smaller than the captain in all counts.

"He is a bloody thief!" cried another, somewhat bigger than the latter, but not by much.

"Throw him into the river!" cheered all the fish together, before the words turned into a chant.

So The Fish of Eck took hold of the old-man and threw him into the river, and for the his ill-fated luck, he did not know how to swim.

Harlot was very much astonished to see that the old-man could not keep himself above the water for even a short period of time, for she was much younger than he and she knew how to do such an activity well enough. The girl also felt quite proud of herself that she was capable of keeping her breath underwater for much longer than he did.

A talented girl indeed!

In any event, the tortoise was not pleased with the suitable outcome of the old-man, and so he made a loud howl like noise, which startled all around and caused every fish to take hostile positions, spears and lilies pointed outward.

"Oh my goodness gracious me!" Harlot cried out, still in a competitive mood. "That was very loud. But I bet I can do better."

And so, as the girl tried on with her own roar, the tortoise pulled out a sac of lemons from one of his pockets, snatched several fish, including the captain, and prepared a fine feast, which was accompanied by a buttery sauce made from the bacon of several tiny pigs. The rest of the fish scattered away in fright at the thought of becoming eaten themselves. When all was prepared, only Harlot and the tortoise shared the meal in each other's company, which lasted an entire night.

CHAPTER VII

A LETTER; A TREE

When the girl finished eating, morning had already come. (You see, she had never had the opportunity to eat so much and such a variety of food before, as she was so accustomed to potato gruel, so she made her meal last as long as she could possibly manage it.) Interestingly enough, the tortoise had already started preparing soft roe and sausages for breakfast, making sure to use up all leftovers from the prior feast; nevertheless, he was the only one who partook, for Harlot's stomach could not be filled anymore for the moment.

When both were done with their eating, each rested and thought. Though the sun went and came, nothing else of note occurred.

Finally, once their legs grew tired of being still, both decided to walk.

It was soon after this event that the tortoise stumbled upon a tattered scroll that laid a few feet under a rock.

"What is it?" pondered the curious girl.

"I believe it is a scroll," replied the tortoise.

"What does it say? I am very much excited to know what it says. Please read it. Please read it now this very instant!" questioned and then commanded Harlot impatiently.

"I believe it is a letter from a quean of Eck to a quean of Ick," told the tortoise.

"How exciting! How many queens are there? Are there only two or are there more than two? Please tell me there are more than two. Oh, it would be so exciting if there were, though quite confusing to understand which queen to follow," babbled the girl.

"It is all the same," appraised the tortoise. "For all I care, there could be twelve queans, one for every hour, each having their own precise time to do whatever they please. Well, I suppose not. That would be unethical to most. Not as they please that is."

"But it would be two hours each," corrected Harlot in an intelligent manner, for she had learnt everything about how to count and calculate time.

"In any case," responded the tortoise, "would you like to hear what the letter says?"

The girl was very much distracted at the thought of queens as well as the tortoise's critical mistake of calculating time that she did not notice when he began to read out loud:

Dear quean of Ick,

I would like to inform you that I have high acknowledgments and very high suspicions that cause me to believe with no doubt of wonder that I wish to say what must be said about my own understanding, for if not, I might soon become withered and pushed aside for hounds to nibble at my bones, which would inevitably create much hysteria within all I have ever believed in.

quean of Eck

"Well that was a useless letter. Nothing? Nothing at all? Absolutely nothing? Nothing?" stated Harlot with intensity.

"Did you expect the letter to be useful?" replied the tortoise, inflating his stereotypical beliefs with such a document as proof.

"This is travesty!" exclaimed the girl.

The tortoise then heard a sound and asked, "What was that noise?"

"What! How dare you speak to me that way. I was talking! I am no noise," declared Harlot.

The sound the tortoise heard repeated itself in a louder loudness this time so that the girl was also able to take notice of it. Now that they both had heard something, they each directed their eyes towards the sound's direction; to their discovery, they discovered a three-foot-tree standing a whole three-feet tall by the side of some sort of bush with things on it.

"Are you the noise, bushwalker?" interrogated the girl.

"Noise. Where about?" spoke the three-foot-tree, twitching its feet, which were roots, from side to side in a neuroses manner.

"Right where you are," replied Harlot.

The three-foot-tree stomped its feet twice, rotated itself in a clockwise direction, then in the opposite direction, all while attempting to leap somewhere somehow.

"What are you doing? If I did not know any better, I would guess that you have eaten much too many sugar drops. Is that it? Oh, I do hope so. I would certainly enjoy a few right now, especially the ones that taste like butterscotch, but the chewy ones, not those hard ones.

Those ones are awful. I really do hope you have some left," the girl questioned and then hoped.

The three-foot-tree voiced nothing in response for some time; instead it stood completely still.

Eventually, the three-foot-tree put forth a question, "Have you always been standing there?"

"Of course not. How could I always be standing here? That is quite a questionable assumption you know," wittingly criticized Harlot, as she was displeased with her dismal chances of getting a sugar drop.

"Is that a letter?" sounded the three-foot-tree onto another matter.

"Yes it is a letter, but it is a terrible letter," informed the girl.

"May I see it?" asked the three-foot-tree.

"Yes, I supposed you may," allowed Harlot.

The three-foot-tree looked deeply into the flat paper and then announced, "No, no, not a thing."

"I agree," agreed the girl.

Harlot quickly went round and stood next to the three-foot-tree to look at the letter to point out its faults. But to her dismay, the letter was upside down with its words on the other side of the paper.

"Why, you have the letter upside down with the letters pointed completely away from your sight," fumed the girl, with a not so hidden tone of anger and frustration.

"What does it matter?" told the three-foot-tree. "I do not wish to read it anyways. It is a nuisance if you ask me."

"It very much matters. You would certainly need the letters of the words facing you top to bottom, left to right, bottom side down. If you do not follow these strict regulations you will certainly be unable to read anything," Harlot stated, as if she was a professor giving a lecture.

"What if I was to see the letter through a looking-glass?" inquired the three-foot-tree.

The girl then attempted to explain how to hold a paper if one was looking at it through a looking-glass: "You would need to hold the bottom side up, wait...no...you would need to hold the bottom side down as usual, but the left side would have to be held on the right, wait...that is not correct either. Oh! I do not care. What is the purpose of reading a paper through a looking-glass in the first place? Oh, never mind."

And so the tortoise read the letter out loud.

Once finished, Harlot and the three-foot-tree spent much time discussing what it could mean (or what it could not mean is perhaps a better way of putting it). After much deliberation, a decision was made between the two that the letter was indeed a letter, but that was all.

The tortoise decided to speak for a while after this, giving an extended sermon about his thoughts on the idea of trying to find any meaning in what was written. Since the girl thought his words to be gibberish, she became annoyed, and so walked in an away direction. To her surprise, neither the three-foot-tree nor the tortoise followed behind her; thus, she continued into that specific direction, while her mind thought away about all sorts of things.

Once it came time that the colours of the land around her began to fade with the sun, Harlot realized that she was completely alone within a lush green meadow.

CHAPTER VIII

A FROG-THING

As the girl looked about, looking this way and that way and another way, she noticed a small wooden structure by the beginning of a bunch of tall and short, small and large tress. The construction was no larger than a common dark closet, but no smaller than a cupboard. (If it pleases you to call this object something in particular, you may do so; I am not sure what to call it myself.) While there was something on the building that looked to be a door, no handle was to be seen anywhere.

Frustrated by the idea, Harlot decided to sit on the ground; yet, at the very moment the girl's bottom touched near the meadow grass, the door of the cabin gladly opened, for she had partially sat on a plank of wood that had slid into an opening then into another connected to the door. With a great sense of accomplishment, she stood up and looked into the unlit abyss that laid unfastened in front of her; sublime some would call it, while others other things.

Nevertheless, she went in without hesitation.

After the first step was taken, then another, Harlot's feet began to feel as if they were getting wetter and wetter. So with the intension of preventing this, for she did not understand why such a thing was happening, the girl tried to step out of the door behind her, but no door lay where it had just been a moment ago; instead, she was standing on a lily pad that was in the process of sinking deeper and deeper into the water beneath her.

"Oh dear! What am I to do?" cried Harlot aloud.

"You must get a h.a.w.p.," spoke a frog-thing that had just come out of a stone.

"Onto what?" questioned the girl, as she continued to sink.

"You must get a h.a.w.p.," spoke the frog-thing once more, before it went on hopping along a path of grey lily pads.

Harlot was awfully concerned by the thought of getting her whole self wet, but not of drowning of coarse. So she hopped from one lily pad to the next, as she thought the frog-thing had informed, finding it all quite amusing.

The frog-thing sang the following as they went along:

H.a.w.p.! H.a.w.p.! H.a.w.p.!
I'll never stopa
I'll never stopa
H.a.w.p.! H.a.w.p.! H.a.w.p.!
T'll I dropa
T'll I dropa
H.a.w.p.! Stop! Flop!
Fill the lungs to the topa
I'll fill the lungs to the topa

Luckily, just as the girl was about to stop her hopping, due to an overwhelming tiredness, she reached the end of the lily pad path. And then there came a Splash! onto the edge of the ripples and wetness covered some of her; but since there was a feeling of relief, she did not mind in the least.

"So did you get a h.a.w.p.?" vainly inquired the frog-thing, who now stood at Harlot's side.

"Oh yes I did indeed. It was so much fun that I wish to do it again. Maybe even again after that, many times. But it was quite tiring. I am not sure I could do it that many times without needing a rest," informed the girl enthusiastically.

Harlot then realized that she was standing by the edge of a moat, which just so happened to surround a magnificent looking castle. To her delight, she had to hop along another line of lily pads in order to get to its Gatehouse.

And so she did, and the frog-thing followed.

"What are those?" asked the girl curiously to the frog-thing once in front of the castle; she was pointing at a wall that held colourful arching leaves with carvings in them.

"Those are called Flying Dutch Dresses," educated the frog-thing. "They are much too small for you to put on and much too big for you to go into." It took a moment of pause before going on. "Each one holds its very own carving of a certain history and event that has taken place around here since the very Beginning. There are various carvings of festivals and games and battles."

"Is there a place for me?" questioned Harlot.

"That's not history," answered the frog-thing.

And sure enough, as the girl looked closely at the carvings in the leaves, she did not see herself engraved, nor would any of Harlot's history ever be deemed as historicity to the eyes of most. In any account, she continued on with her search, looking upon the recorded past through the eyes of the victor.

"That is boring history. This one too. Oh, what is that one right there? It is so pretty, like fresh berries squished into a glass jar," told, then questioned, and then again told the girl with much interest.

"That's the carving of Weaple the Beatle," informed the frog-thing in a shocked and utterly surprised manner. "You mean to say that you do not know who he is, or even the story of Weaple the Beatle for that matter?"

Harlot felt quite embarrassed that she did not know the details of such an important figure. Thus, to relieve some awkwardness, she mixed her words around and did not tell the truth to its whole or the whole of the truth or the truth with no holes.

And so the girl replied, "I do not seem to be able to remember at the moment."

The frog-thing enjoyed telling tales very much, so it became quite excited by the opportunity, and this is what it told: "In a place where…umm—"

"A what? An umm? Stories that start with umms are always the most dreadfully boring," interjected Harlot, speaking in a way that insinuated the frog-thing did not know anything about its history lesson.

"Well…umm," the frog-thing continued to struggle. "Oh dear. There was a beetle who…who…well, his name was Weaple…and…well…I do believe I have forgot. It has something to do about this beetle and a quean; yes, that is for sure. And also, something about a man and a can and a head; he now lives in the castle."

"I do believe your story is quite the lecture," told the girl, rather bored.

"Well…" began the frog-thing. "Ha! I remember. The man fancies boxes, very peculiar ones. And…ah yes, and it has been said that if someone should present him with a box that he…well something in those lines, that he will give to whomever he pleases all of his possessions."

Harlot shouted with much excitement at the idea, for she had often theorized about putting together a variety of boxes, especially those that could be flipped from side to side for multipurpose uses.

She believed that there was no doubt her box would please the man and so own all he had.

It was all quite exciting to her.

CHAPTER IX

AN UNFOURTUNATE INCIDENT WITH THE SPRIGGANS

Meanwhile, the three-foot tree and the tortoise were very much confused with their present situation; at one moment they were having a splendid conversation, which counted three, but now there were only two.

"I think there needs to be an explanation for this," told the three-foot-tree to the tortoise.

"No, no," returned the tortoise. "Nothing of the such is necessary. Though it is ill-timed."

The three-foot-tree then began to fidget, paired with the rubbing of its branches, almost enough to let out a brush of smoke, all the while looking as if it was trying to place itself somewhere somehow.

Then it stopped and asked a question: "Have you always been standing there?"

And so, after a not so quick conversation (which I do not feel the need of writing down, since it was indeed a futile conversation, and if it were not for what happened next I do believe would have never ended) the two began to walk unknowingly into the same direction Harlot had wondered off moments ago.

It just so happened that a scrawny-man came floundering by with the sounds of surrounding bells. Behind him followed a barrow, which he struggled about with pride.

The contraption was pilled with occupants, all sharing matching tokens, similar to the ones upon his neck.

"That's a mighty tale today," asserted the tortoise to the scrawny-man as they came side-by-side, though not too close.

"I suppose it is," replied the scrawny-man in a tone. "Though, it can take a few more."

"We should make a few cheers and have a tiddly," proposed the three-foot-tree.

"If no other cure arises, other than my beak and the ring around my wrist, that is all we shall do," answered the scrawny-man. "Though I have already had a enough Lambs Wool to cover a heard," he continued, "I always have room for more." He paused and then began again. "As the good man says, 'Let them fall and let Him sort them out.'"

"Cheers!" called the three-foot-tree.

"Cheers!" sounded the other two.

Silence followed.

"Well I must be off," told the scrawny-man. "I don't want them getting too cold for my taste."

Yet, as the scrawny-man began to begin to set about on his way, a band of horrid looking Spriggans came surrounding the three travellers from every side, which caused quite a ruckus.

"Is this your doing?" snarled one creature, pointing at the occupants of the carriage.

"It has to be," growled another beast. "I saw it happen with my own eyes. They poisoned the well. Now we cannot drink. We will all die because of them."

At this moment, the three-foot-tree, the scrawny-man, and the tortoise became fairly worried, for the unpleasant looking things did not look or sound gracious of their company.

The Spriggans' ugly bodies were contorted and crocked in every way imaginable, and unimaginable; as for their mouths, they bore cracked teeth and fat tongues. Their skin and bones were mostly black and brown with dried red crust upon their feet, knees, and fingertips. Each beast wore a different shaped hat made of all sorts of things. Some carried their hats upon their heads, while others on their shoulders. Some hats were obnoxiously tall, while others looked so short they seemed to go straight down into their heads. Some went far to one side and some to the other, while others wore hats that were entirely strange altogether.

"What is it you believe we have done?" questioned the scrawny-man.

"You have stolen from the Hollows and made interest with your earnings," gargled one creature that was much uglier than the rest.

"Stolen what from the Hollows?" asked the tortoise, while keeping a calm figure.

"You know what you have stolen," shouted the contorted Spriggan, while moving closer and closer to the three unfortunate comrades. "Do not act is if you are unaware of what I say, peck of a meal. Hi hi hoy hoy hoy! It is hearsay I say!" The creature stopped and then continued in a rather cheerful but wicked tone, "Oh yes, let us introduce our intentions."

The ugly thing moved back to where the others of his kind were cluttered and then pulled out two small sticks, which he began to beat together in a rhythmic tone. Half of the rest of the lot began to hum in low assorted voices while the rest stomped their feet. A smaller, but just as repulsive creature, who went unnoticed before, stepped forward. The hat it wore was a silver crown, which held flint rocks at the edge of each point. There were six points in total. One looked a little worn. No one was sure why. Also, it wore the crown upon its head.

The small Spriggan sang these lyrics to a musical ensemble in a somber voice with the rest of the creatures, who all chanted with him at the last part of the verse, which escalated louder and more uncivilized with each repetition:

Tick tock
Wobble frock
Up to the gallows
Up on the rock
There goes the triggerman
Drop! Drop! Drop!

What a passionate lot of Spriggans. They must have repeated the verse a good thirty-three and a half times. It was a frightening sight to see, nevertheless an inspiring one.

"Since you have now heard our design," spoke the creature that had been the main attraction, "we now command you to build us something like a holding cage for yourselves so we may take you wherever we chose."

"Wie wee," shuddered another repugnant creature that was salivating silver saliva, and had no nose. "Perhaps they shall get a…" at this moment the beast made a clap noise with its hands, "and a bite from a little blind visiting waterbird. Achoo! Snort! Snort! Achoo!"

"Keep the goose bumps to yourself!" snapped the smaller Spriggan, as he came and stood in front of the one who had just spoken. "They will be untouched until we all make a consensus on what to do with them."

Talking ceased and the three-foot-tree, the scrawny-man, and the tortoise built a fashionable device, much like a pushcart, but with bars to keep the prisoners contained.

And then they were off.

It was a bumpy as well as an unpleasant ride, as there was a constant array of burning things thrown into the captives' direction, as well as ceaseless gibes. The scrawny-man's luck was eventually pressed beyond its limit: The beasts ate all of his fingers and toes, and then he lost his noes; he did not make the journey beyond the third night.

As the darkness of the forth night was suppressed and morning came forth, the three-foot-tree and the tortoise became very hungry and much aggravated by the lack of progression in their journey of imprisonment. There was also much bickering and brawling and brannigans throughout the clan of Spriggans; hence the lack of distance travelled and the lack of headway.

"I crave nourishment inside of me," announced the three-foot-tree, refraining itself to a speech. "Oh how I wish I could remember the warmth of the sun upon my branches and the earth between my roots. Let us feed; even if only for a moment, I would be satisfied."

You see, not only was the pushcart uncomfortable, but it was also a dark and dismal place to be within. They had sadly built their imprisonment for aesthetics sake and not for comfort.

"It is no use," responded the tortoise. "These cruel creatures have no understanding of mercy. They seem to have fallen far from the Tree of Grace, or perhaps too near."

"But what are we to do then?" inquired the three-foot-tree.

"Quite your chatter!" attacked an unknown voice from an unknown place.

"What was that?" inquired an ugly Spriggan to another.

"What was what?" responded the other.

"I heard a voice, or something of the sort," answered the first.

"Arm yourselves and be ready," shouted an armored fish on the back of a tiny pig that had suddenly appeared on the path the Spriggans were travelling upon. "Those prisoners are ours. Let them go at once so we may take them captive."

It was no other than the army of The Fish of Eck, ready to take revenge for their eaten comrades. The rest of the army followed behind the fish that had spoken; he, the new captain, as the last, was the largest fish, had the largest spear, largest water lily, largest flower, and sat on the largest tiny pig.

"Shout!" shouted the captain, which caused the entire army to take their orderly positions and then shout out all together.

The ugliest Spriggan approached the fish that was in charge and then spoke while slobbering over the tiny pig. "You fool, these are our prisoners and you will never have them."

"You are wrong," exclaimed the captain. "We will have them no matter the price. I make you this promise."

"Well then," replied the ugly creature, "you will have to destroy us all if you wish to have them."

And so, at the same moment, both sides yelled out and attacked one another.

There were spears, stones, and other dangerous things thrown left and right; an epic battle it was. The Spriggans grew into their notorious giant like forms, while the fish used their little pigs to get around and about with ease. There was much blood spilt on both sides. Yet in the end, both The Fish of Eck and the Spriggans experienced what seemed to be total defeat.

The three-foot-tree and the tortoise were filled with utter joy to see all the dead bodies lying about, for it meant their freedom. After exiting the cart, which had been somewhat destroyed due to the battle, they took their liberty and celebrated: The three-foot-tree smoked his marble pipe stuffed with cotton wax embers and the tortoise made a rich fish stew with some of the pig trotters he found upon the ground.

After this they continued on, still unknowingly heading into the same direction the girl had taken not long ago. (You see, the Spriggans had really not made that much of a distance.) The two also ended up in the same lush green meadow as Harlot had, but it was now covered by a carnival.

CHAPTER X

A BIRD THAT FLEW AWAY, AND OTHER EXPLANATIONS

Before going on any further, the pair noticed a small white glowing pebble lying upon the ground. The tortoise picked it up, examined it, and then gave it to the three-foot-tree. The three-foot-tree examined it and then gave it back to the tortoise. The tortoise then tried to put the pebble into his pocket, but the pebble was much too hot to lay bare inside. So the tortoise wrapped it in moss and tossed it aside.

After the notable event, the two followed a path that led straight through the carnival's core. There were lights and sounds and many other things happening all about: this and that and this and that.

Eventually, the travellers made their way to a caged bird that wore metal wings upon its back. The extensions on the creature looked very much useless, for they seemed to anchor the thing flat onto its chest and stomach; it was as if the bird would have a difficult time to simply tip-toe a half length of hay.

In the beast wagon next to the bird was something like a mog, one completely fabricated out of all different types of scrapes of metals and woods. It did not seem of the cheerful sort, for a sore smile was placed upon its face.

"What is the matter?" inquired the three-foot-tree to the mog-made-of-scrapes-of-metals-and-woods.

The mog-made-of-scrapes-of-metals-and-woods raised its head and then answered in a low gloomy voice, "I am lonely and I do not appreciate entrapment behind these bars for another's amusement." It stopped for a moment, sneezed, and then continue, "I am doomed to be sad as long as I live."

"That sounds ghastly," agreed the tortoise.

"It is indeed," granted the mog-made-of-scrapes-of-metals-and-woods.

The three-foot-tree's trunk then began to twitch, while its roots stretched out as far as they possible could; this continued on while it scratched itself all over, seemingly trying to do something somehow.

"Have you always been standing there?" asked the three-foot-tree.

The mog-made-of-scrapes-of-metals-and-woods paid no attention to the question and naturally laid its head back down onto its front metal paws, supporting the heavy weight of its head; there seemed to be nothing more the three-foot-tree nor the tortoise could do for the sad looking moggie. Thus, the spectators continued on with their goings through and through the carnival.

They saw wonderful things all about them, such as a Picture Gallery with eleven fingers and several Pickled Punks without any at all; indeed the work of an Incubus they thought. There were also tall things, skinny things, short things, and fat things, and many other different things, not one the same. But the pair grew jaded of walking and so wondered what else could be done for their amusement besides looking.

"What do you suppose we do?" pondered the tortoise out loud.

"I would love to play a game and win some fancy prize," answered the three-foot-tree.

But there was no time for a game or even two, for an announcement had been made, one much louder then was needed, demanding everyone to sit: a grand show was about to begin. The three-foot-tree and the tortoise followed the speaker's instructions and placed themselves upon provided porcelain seats within a small, empty, soft-lot. They were very much excited and anticipated entertainment, which began after a little teaser curtain fell away into the ground.

"What a selfish curtain," declared the three-foot-tree, refraining itself to a speech. "All this time it oppressed such a small though magnificent stage. A stage that has a floor made of wood from the bodies of my own and others. And look, to the right and to the left, there are little buildings, all made of porcelain, or something, just like our seats. Oh joyous times! Such an event as this demands something, something... Look, something is making its way onto the stage."

And so it had been, and so there was.

A Gaffer, who was quite thin, with one long neck, two long ears, and three long arms, swayed into their sights, left and then right repeated, like a gumdrop stuck upon a grand-clock's pendulum. At some points, it appeared as if the thin man would fall onto one of his sides completely, for his head swayed ever so close to the ground. The Gaffer wore bright clothing and round dark footwear.

As the performance commenced, all that could be seen from the viewpoint of the spectators was the performer placed in the middle of the stage, swaying, and busy about. There was cooking and cutting and basting and baking and brushing and other things as well.

When the Gaffer stopped what he was doing, he sent out a question, "Can someone tell me what this is?"

(It was a Question Mark Show you see.)

"I can tell you what it is!" shouted the three-foot-tree, almost cracking the seat underneath its roots.

The long-necked man continued to look into the crowed, if two can be called such a thing, and asked the question once again, trying to find his mark.

The three-foot-tree then shouted with all its might, being it was it's favourite thing to put into a pipe: "A Goose Berry flavoured Water-Drop!"

This time the three-foot-tree's seat did break a little: And so, the little piece of porcelain that had been segregated by will, or perhaps ostracized by force from its community, went soaring out into the vast world of the lot. The porcelain piece eventually grew into a porcelain tree and bared porcelain fruit that was eaten by a famished bear that turned into porcelain itself and eventually tripped over a log and broke its head on the very tree it had eaten the porcelain fruit from.

Though the three-foot-tree took no notice of the porcelain piece, it was nevertheless the sign of a chalky pat of the hand upon the back for the Gaffer.

Explanation of the item, a Water-Drop: A Water-Drop is water that has been prepared, using distinctive techniques, into a firm jelly like ball, which inevitably allows an ease in transportation. The jelly ball can be turned back into its liquid form by puncturing its precise centre with a cotton string. Yet, if a Water-Drop is heated up, it turns into a waxy substance that slowly dissolves into a velvet like mist, which is well suited for the inside of one's mouth. The jelly and wax forms are the finest ways to consume water, for drinking it in its liquid state is very plain and uninteresting.

"Indeed it is, my mooch," replied the long-eared man. "It would then appear that you know that this is no cheap paste."

"I suppose I do," responded the three-foot-tree rather calmly.

The performer came down from the stage, swaying with every step, made himself right in front of the three-foot-tree and the tortoise, and then inquired, "What would you offer for such a delicious Water-Drop?"

The three-foot-tree was very much determined to get its prize and so offered up all its items of worth at once, none of which were trimmed.

The Gaffer became quite excited by the simplicity of getting his mark to stake all of its possessions with a simple shake of a squash rake, but continued on calmly, smoothly taking a silver chain out from his front pocket and a nearby box that had been used for a recent Revue show, so to play something sure to please.

Explanation of the game, Pricking the Garter: A shackle is to be wrapped around a box; it is then to be pulled virtuously tight so that both hold securely within their place, even if tempted to move. Within the middle, the form of an X, or some sort of such rippled shape, is to be found. On the one side of the X, one may take a guess to poke their prick, hoping that it will hold within and find a breeding bounty. However, the chance is half and half, for on the other side of the X, one's prick will surely meet with nothing but the slipping of the chain, though the ending of the event will come nonetheless, perhaps a more desired finale.

(This was the game, and this is as it has always been played.)

Thus, the three-foot-tree stood still, spending much time in contemplation, thinking and thinking the situation over: the prick it planed to place was one of much thought and consideration, and thus much time was deserved to be spent so that the correct decision was made (a rare breed).

This continued on, then on, then on some more.

After continuously coxing the three-foot-tree to make a selection, the long-armed man realized that his mark was well beyond his ability, one who spent hours in strategy, and was also a vacuous laggard. Thus, by irritable happenstance, the Gaffer gave up on his mark, left the prize, took his collection from the brief Blowoff, then swayed away.

The three-foot-tree was very much in high spirits and proud of itself, for it had won the game without even finishing its thoughts; the Goose Berry flavoured Water-Drop was put away for safekeeping.

The two then decided to do some more sightseeing.

Since the carnival was quite restrictive in its circumference area, one that was easily explorable within but a few minutes, the two shortly made their way back to the metal winged bird and the mog-made-of-scrapes-of-metals-and-woods, where the three-foot-tree made high and low pitched noises while swaying its branches in a manner that looked like it was trying to be somewhere somehow; it then inquired once becoming still, "Have you always been standing there?"

A response from itself about something else came however.

"Yes that is it," gwayled the three-foot-tree. "I know what to do."

Explanation of the word, gwayled: Though the word 'gwayled,' there are no variants, such as gwayle or gwaylness, cannot be found within a current English dictionary, it is indeed a word. Such a word can be used in moments of excitement, confusion, or even times of sadness. It can be used as a verb, a noun, a compliment, or anything in between. Put simply, 'gwayled' can be utilized whenever one thinks it best fits within a written sentence or even when using spoken words.

"Tell us," insisted the tortoise. "I suppose if you must."

"I do not care to hear," told the mog-made-of-scrapes-of-metals-and-woods in a pessimistic manner, "for I know I am forever doomed and nothing will ever bring me any sort of benefit."

The three-foot-tree spoke anyways, "We should look underneath the Beast wagon to see if there is a Belly Box with a key inside."

So they looked.

And indeed there was a Belly Box where the three-foot-tree had supposed one to be, next to where a possum-belly-quean had been sleeping not long ago. And sure enough, there was a key within, the Belly Box that is, but it so happened to only open the cage of the bird.

"I am doomed," announced the mog-made-of-scrapes-of-metals-and-woods, in its usual miserable sounding voice. "But I have expected and have accepted my fate. Go and live your lives and forget about me for as long as you may live. Things will be better that way."

During the speech, the metal winged creature had freed itself, and to everyone's surprise, the bird flew away.

"Isn't that odd," told the mog-made-of-scrapes-of-metals-and-woods.

"Yes," voiced the three-foot-tree.

"Indeed," acknowledged the tortoise. "I was under the impression that its wings were as useful as no wings at all."

And then, just as the three-foot-tree and tortoise were about to make their separate ways from the mog-made-of-scrapes-of-metals-and-woods once again, a great gust of wind came sweeping by, carrying a great deal of hay and dirt with it, completely covering the cage, it's contents, and all three travellers. All laid stuck underneath the deep heap of debris for some time, while the carnival folk just so happened to pack their things and travel away; since the cage was disguised, it was not seen, and thus not taken.

When all managed to make themselves unstuck, and the field was once again empty, no words were spoken about the happening. The three comrades simply went on with their day, searching for something to eat while reading the midway as they went along: The tortoise found a few bushes of round Mud Berries and a few Glass Berries, while the three-foot-tree ate some dirt and later enjoyed its pipe with a piece of the newly acquired Goose Berry flavored Water-Drop in it. The mog-made-of-scrapes-of-metals-and-woods ate nothing, for everyone knows that mogs do not eat.

Explanation of the first edibles, Mud Berries: Mud berries are ugly looking berries. They are pale in colour and atrocious in sent, but some enjoy their tangy bitter taste. The plant itself is often mistaken for a muddy puddle, but it is much tougher in texture when tasted. The berry is what gives the plant its distinct identity, as it looks like a mix between a pile of sawdust and that of well-used rags.

Explanation of the second edibles, Glass Berries: Glass Berries are quite the opposite from Mud Berries. The stem of the plant is made of pure white snuff, while its black coloured leaves are a mix of wild sunflower honey, molasses, and maple syrup. The berry of this plant looks like an over sized raindrop, which has a sweet and creamy taste (as well as other traits I do not think it appropriate to write, for I would indeed do it no justice).

When the time for eating had come to an end, the three-foot-tree, the mog-made-of-scrapes-of-metals-and-woods, and the tortoise noticed a small wooden property not far off in the distance, and so they made themselves to one of its sides.

Since they believed there to be nothing of particular use on this side, they all went to another side, hoping not to be disappointed again. As fate would have it, they were not in the least, for something like a door laid before them. Though no handle was to be seen, after much a conversation, it was decided that the three-foot-tree was to push its branches into the door and break it open by force.

It did, and the door was opened.

The three-foot-tree, the mog-made-of-scrapes-of-metals-and-woods, and the tortoise all walked into whatever was in front of them, one after another.

CHAPTER XI

OBSERVATIONS INSIDE A CASTLE

As Harlot continued to stand, still thinking of box making, she soon overcame the specific thought and noticed that in-between two slender towers was a front gate, and it laid splendidly open; so she pleasurably entered between with ease.

Once within, the girl took notice of her many surroundings:

Oh how the-man-with-a-can-for-a-head's castle was quite an attractive marvel. For one, there were no ceilings; instead of such contemporary designs, clouds were relied upon to keep one dry from the sun. And, upon these clouds hung embroidered chandeliers made of wax and orange peels, which were held together and hung by continuously hemming cobwebs. Though a practical design, the lighting was known to become quite bothersome in the evenings, for whenever the clouds moved, so did the light of the chandeliers; sometimes they even floated away completely, and when that happened, darkness had the last say.

With further observations, Harlot noticed oddly placed stonewalls doing nothing particularly useful.

In other places, around here and there, were trees of every sort and ponds of every shape. Many of both made themselves into spirals, while the remaining ones were skinny, then fat, or fat, and then skinny.

In other places were clay structures with wooden stairs, ones which seemed to lead somewhere in the up and down directions.

In other other places dimness populated so that nothing could be clearly seen.

As the girl did her looking about, suddenly, without a warning, or even a polite introduction, she noticed that little holes had made their way into her dress, and more hoped to do the same. Naturally, a game of tag began; Harlot knew they wanted to land upon her flesh, but she did mind losing a limb from such a meeting, so she ran from them in a prompt manner.

After much distress, and a bit of fun of course, a few more holes had made themselves into her dress; but when tiredness took over the pursuers, the girl was able to carry on with her observations of the castle.

And she soon found herself in front of a hollow black tree that was in the process of turning back into dirt; it was covered in sharp, long, yellow needles.

"I wonder if they are sharp," wondered the curious Harlot aloud.

So brave as she was, she put her hands upon a vacant bushel of bodkins with an impressive force, but the needles merely went straight through her hands without making a feeling; though there was disappointment, she accepted not having been pricked.

While there were many other things to look at, such as roaming feathered creatures with necks as tall as a hundred chocolate cakes, all piled on top one another with extra thick cream, each and each placed on every layer, the girl noticed that her hands felt unusually heavy.

"Why, I do believe my hands are beginning to feel as if they were covered in mud, or stone, or even rain," thought Harlot as she examined the present sensations of those extremities.

Yet, to the girl's surprise, when she looked down at her hands, there were no hands to be seen. They had disappeared entirely.

"My goodness gracious me!" shouted the handless Harlot with disgust.

The girl then turned around in circles, sat down, got back up, and then sighed. She was very upset.

"How am I to eat, or put on my clothes, or even scratch myself when I become itchy? This is just terrible, just terrible," pleaded Harlot to her body.

"Don't fuss about such unimportant things," lectured the frog-thing who had been quite absent from all the happenings and sights. "Look over there."

And so the girl did.

And what she saw was another hollow tree, but this one was covered in tiny red eyes and purple horseshoes. Since the eyes seemed to be looking at Harlot with much interest, she tried to pick one out. However, the realization quickly came that such a task would not be likely, for there were no hands around to pick things out with; also, the girl could hardly raise the places where those departed pieces use to be even if there looked to no longer be anything left to lift.

This caused a great deal of frustration. To calm her rattled nerves, she placed herself into a squash-shaped pond;

while the water did feel a little hotter than she liked, it nevertheless made the situation seem more bearable.

It was then that Harlot remarked a pumpkin sitting next to a mortar and pestle right at the edge of the pond. She was quite fond of mortars and pestles, so to create a moment of amusement she put the pumpkin in the mortar and ground it with the pestle.

"My goodness, my hands are back and no longer feel heavy," exclaimed the girl in much delight when she realized she was able to use the pestle.

"Well that is obvious," told the frog-thing. "That's a hand growing pond. There is even a sign right next to it that reads,

-HAND GROWING POND-

Don't you see it?"

Harlot was much more interested in stirring the pestle than listening to the frog-thing and its boring lectures, so she paid no attention to it.

As she stirred on, the scent of the pumpkin mush became more and more invigorating. Yet, it did not smell anything like pumpkin; instead, a fragrance of a fine braggot brew filled the air. Enjoying the smell ever so much, the girl took the pumpkin remains and put them into the pond with her; she then spun around with her arms spread open, mixing the water like a great delectable potion. However, what had been sensually enjoyable soon came to an end; for when all had been blended together, a black and foul liquid came to be.

Harlot laughed and laughed some more; it was as if someone had told her a very humorous joke.

"What are you laughing at?" asked the much confused frog-thing.

"Why, it looks like that black onion soup. What a terrible tasting concoction. It is just awful," preached the girl.

"We should get going on to see the-man-with-a-can-for-a-head," insisted the frog-thing. "Wouldn't you agree?"

"Agree, or not. Achoo!" responded Harlot.

"I suppose," answered the frog-thing.

The girl found the frog-thing to be quite annoying with its recent responses, so she stumbled off and away from it, and soon ended up in front of a sign next to a staircase that read,

-TO THE LEFT YOU CANNOT GO
TO THE RIGHT IS NO BETTER-

"Well that is a useless sign. Useless," mocked Harlot.

"And why is that?" questioned the frog-thing, after it had caught up to her.

"Because a rock is blocking the way on the left and a wall on the right. Even if I wanted to go left or right, I would not be able too. If I wanted to go into another direction than the one I came from, the only way to go is up those stairs that lay straight ahead," cleverly explained the girl.

Thus up and up the stairs they both went, and a long time it took is very much the truth. The staircase seemed to be never ending, for there was the impression that there would be another twist or turn at every next moment.

The following is the logic the frog-thing used to explain this never-ending-ness, which it voiced out loud: "If a blind bird was to walk up a staircase with the intension of reaching a known place, it may simply walk up the staircase to go wherever that may be. But if that same blind bird was to walk up a staircase without knowing what was to be found on the other side, or what it wanted to find, how would it know if it ever got to where it wanted to go, or if it got anywhere at all?"

After a long and exhausting climb, both were relieved when they reached the top of the eventual ending staircase; the frog-thing's theory was now useless.

There was a door with a sign that read,

-THIS IS…
THE DOOR…
THAT LEADS TO…
THE-MAN-WITH-A-CAN-FOR-A-HEAD-

"Now that's providence," declared the frog-thing.
Harlot said nothing to this remark.

CHAPTER XII

After making their way inside, the two found themselves in a small hallway made completely out of clay doors. Each door looked identical, with the exception of the fact that they were all different colours.

"I count eight doors," announced the girl, trying to show her counting abilities.

There were however more than eight doors, for Harlot had forgotten to look in the upwards and downwards directions.

"There are sixteen doors," corrected the frog-thing. "Don't forget to look up and down."

The girl acted as if she had not heard a word the frog-thing had said; a few moments later she made the following known: "Aha! Correction. There are eight doors on the walls and four doors upon the ceiling and four doors upon the floor. That makes a total of sixteen doors. We shall open the red door first."

And so they did; this one was on a wall.

As the door was made of clay, with the addition of the rooms' dampness, a simple turn of the handle turned the door into a pile of tart shaped puzzle pieces. To Harlot's pleasure, behind the door laid two pieces of black toast hanging from a collection of strings; this was the manner of toast in which the girl very much enjoyed to eat, and so she gobbling them both up immediately on sight.

"That was a wonderful door. I hope all of the other doors are just like this one. We shall open the green door next," rejoiced and then ordered Harlot.

After turning the handle of the next door, it also crumbled away; this one was hiding a pair of black thorn sown boots.

"I've always wanted boots," announced the frog-thing with much joy.

"I suppose you may have them then," allowed the girl, though feeling jealous.

The frog-thing put the black boots on its back two feet and they fit perfectly.

"We will open the white door upon the ground now," told Harlot.

Since the white door was by the girl's feet, she bent herself over, turned its handle, and then watched as it caved in and away from her.

"I do like what is behind this door very much and must have it," exclaimed Harlot, before she even had time to move the clay aside and see what was underneath.

There was a little black bucket made of a delicate metal substance.

"The black door next, the black door. I want something else," shouted the girl with much excitement.

Inconveniently, the black door had suddenly made its way onto the ceiling. This dilemma caused Harlot to become entangled in great thought.

"You must get a h.a.w.p.," spoke the frog-thing.

Yet, deep in contemplation, the girl ignored the words; so the frog-thing hopped and found itself upon the ceiling as if it was the ground Harlot was standing upon. The girl saw what had happened, and then thought and thought some more; eventually, she was directly next to the frog-thing, next the black door upon the ground.

With a voice expressing achievement through intelligence, Harlot announced, "Very good. Now, let us open the door. I am very much interested in seeing what lies behind it."

However, this time, when the handle was turned, the door fell apart upwards instead of in a downwards direction.

"Oh dear," spoke the frog-thing, who was now staring at a large bedroom below.

"I will go first," insisted the brave girl, who then rashly leaped towards a large bed that lay straight underneath her, with bucket in hand.

The frog-thing followed.

Interestingly enough, Harlot did not simply land on top of the soft looking bed sheets; instead, she found herself underneath them, all of them, which were so thick and so heavy that no light was able to break through.

"It is quite dark in here," asserted the clustered girl to herself.

And it was.

The sheets pressed down upon her little body like heavy bags of flour, causing her lungs to feel quite empty. She sucked about for any air willing to make itself inside her, hoping to fill her lungs enough to carry on; but Harlot was quite aware that she would not last long underneath the sheets if this continued, even though she was able to hold her breath for quite some time under water. Thus, she placed herself onto her hands and knees and moved her body to anyplace that was willing to take her inside.

The girl went forward, legs bent, arms extended, sliding limbs back and forth, sometimes placing herself upon her elbows, sometimes upon her shoulders, sometimes beyond her face, all the while pulling and pushing onwards, looking quite like a pear shaped cream puff, dripping ever so much from the stuffiness and heat of it all.

"I think I see an opening. No, it is not. Wait, yes…it is. Look, over there," rejoiced the determined Harlot.

At last she found her way out from under the heavy bedclothes and laid herself upon a floor.

The frog-thing happened to already be there.

"Hmmm… Yes yes, how do you do?" questioned a composed voice from somewhere nearby. "Tell me, how do you do?"

It was the-man-with-a-can-for-a-head, though the girl did not immediately discern that it was indeed this particular man.

"Hmmm… Yes yes, how do you do?" asked the-man-with-a-can-for-a-head once more, for he was given no answer the first time.

"How do you do?" returned Harlot, feeling annoyed that she had been asked the same question so many times.

"Hmmm… Yes yes, I, I…see," struggled the man. "I, I…see."

Now, since the girl became so irritated with all the repetitions, she did not take the time to observe what the-man-with-a-can-for-a-head looked like; therefore, the following is what she would have seen if she had observed, including her surroundings:

The-man-with-a-can-for-a-head measured about fifteen inches high. One might think of him as a child dwarf man with the exception of having a can for a head, which was the colour of black and was made of cast iron. He wore a red and brown-checkered shirt, light brown trousers, and large stubby brownish black iron toed boots.

The floor of the room was made of brownish wood and the walls were made of red and green sea stones. There were several black wardrobes placed about as decoration, which each held windows that displayed a woodland. The room was elegant as well as teasing, for many puckish paintings and portraits of beautiful beings laid upon the walls, which Harlot would not have recognized if she had taken the time to look at them.

Eventually the girl spoke, "You have quite a large bed."

"Hmmm… Yes yes," answered the man. "So I do."

"But you are so very small. Why do you need such a big bed? I am not sure how you ever manage to find your way out when you wake up each morning. Even I had some difficulty and I am much bigger than you," inquired and then told Harlot.

"Hmmm… Yes yes," replied the the-man-with-a-can-for-a-head. "Why are you here?"

"I came to present to you a box of coarse and then take everything you own for myself. I am quite fond of becoming a queen you know," told the girl bluntly.

The man licked his mouth and took a moment for himself, after which he murmured, "Hmmm… Yes yes, show me your box?"

"Why I need to make it first," educated Harlot.

"Hmmm… Yes yes, you mean to say I will not see your box immediately?" probed the-man-with-a-can-for-a-head with his question.

"Of course not, I intend to prepare one this very instant," informed the girl.

"Hmmm… Yes yes," began the-man-with-a-can-for-a-head. "Since you will not show me your box immediately I have no other choice than to throw you and the other thing into the bottom of my private well. Sentinels! Throw them both in at once. Thank you. Take the bucket and boots from them as well."

And with those words a swarm of tiny men with pick axes, dressed in a similar fashion as their master, came out from behind a door and managed to cause Harlot and the frog-thing to fall into the-man-with-a-can-for-a-head's private well. However, the bucket was not taken, only the frog-thing's boots and a tear of fabric from the girl's dress.

Harlot sat confused at the bottom of a dark and dried up hole.

"That liar! That cheater! I wanted all of his possession and become a queen," hissed the nerved girl.

"What do we do now?" asked the frog-thing, quite upset from the loss of its boots.

"I am not sure, but this well is dry and so I am very pleased that I did not get wet," observed and told Harlot.

It was then that the girl noticed that one of her feet felt different, though she did not know the reason why. After inspection, she discovered that her black bucket had fallen and placed itself on top of her left foot. Yet, when she removed it, she found no foot underneath.

"My goodness, where did it go?" exclaimed Harlot.

With the intension of getting the piece of her body back, she put her hand then arm inside of the bucket, but they too vanished. With the same intention, the girl put her other hand then arm inside of the bucket, but they too met with the same fate. Then, desperately, Harlot inserted the rest of herself until her little body was no longer there.

The frog-thing followed.

CHAPTER XIII

INSIDE THE PLACE OF THE GROUND FAERIES

Swish! Swash! Swumph!!!

Swish! Swash! Swumph!!!

What strange noises Harlot's body did make as her parts tried to put themselves back together again; since there was much flinging, cracking, popping, slapping, and whirling, again and again and again, and even then some more, she eventually succeeded in putting herself back together again quite nicely.

The frog-thing was nowhere to be seen.

Once the process had come to a finish, and the girl's eyes were back in their rightful places, she was able to peek at what marvelous things surrounded her, and this is what she saw: There were all sorts of trees, everywhere around, each filled to the tip of every branch with round and pointy leaves; small caves were placed upon the walls, each covered with glowing lights that only sweet stars could make; there were waterfalls here and there, which flowed into clear crystal streams; every piece of ground was stuffed with the softest, most delicious looking grass one could ever imagine; the air within the underground cavern was delectable to all of the senses, and was quite possibly the finest air Harlot had ever experienced in her entire life.

Though there was even more that excited her.

All around the cave, scattered about ever so nicely, were attractive looking fae beings, Ground Fairies to be exact, whose enticing attributes and presence made the girl's legs and self quiver ever so much that she fell to the ground.

At the sight of the welcomed presence, the pretty beings began to girdle Harlot one by one. Some of them came by air, while others came by foot. Each wore a pair of delicate wings made of autumned-tree-leaves, which were sown onto their backs then sewn together with red and green skkcere-vines. (Though most Faeries are born with wings, Ground Faeries are not.) The clothes upon their bodies were so elegant looking that they could have only been made from the finest of materials and put together by only the most precise of needles.

Yet, one being, whose voice was so elegant that the alluring dress hidding herself was obviously and utterly plain in comparison, asked, "Who may you be?"

The girl was hesitant to speak at first, for the many little women, who also wore differing crowns upon their heads, began to climb up and down her body, looking at her with much interest.

"My name is Harlot," spoke Harlot, feeling quite giddy from all the movement.

"Humph," sounded a little winged one who was lying upon the girl's stomach. "I'm dreadfully bored. Too much chatter. Let's play."

"I know of a game to play. It is a very exciting game. There is one player who runs around trying to touch others and then when they touch someone else they then both have to try and touch everyone else who has not yet been touched until everyone has been touched," explained the girl, very much excited by the opportunity of playing a game in such a place.

"All right," agreed another little woman who wore a rose crown upon her head. "I'll start."

And round and round they all went excitedly, touching one another until every last one had been touched.

"Now what?" asked the Ground Faerie who seemed to get bored quite easily.

"Let us play once more! I had so much fun the first time; I want to play a second," insisted Harlot, rather out of breath but in high spirits.

"No! I want to play Hurling," cried a fae far more beautiful than the one who had been complaining.

"I have never heard of that game before. I rather play a different game. If not the game we have just played then perhaps hot cuckold. Yes, that would be amusing!" told the girl.

"How dare you heckle me while I'm speaking," snarled the pretty woman, feeling ruddily interrupted. "Silence yourself!"

As the moment became heated with passions of all sorts, another occurrence occurred: Everything within the cavern began to shake, while the Faeries began to cry and moan, exhibiting various emotions.

Then round and away went the little bodies, until each one had either hidden inside one of the small caves or had turned into pools of water to be soaked into the earth. Harlot stood alone and annoyed as everyone had left her without even a simple explanation, or even a good-bye, but her mind soon went somewhere else.

Up at the very top where the stones of the ceilings met, was one of the most beautiful and wonderful looking beings the girl had ever seen. The marvel was indeed the colour of white, and not another colour, and there was no physical resemblance to a baby cat, so Harlot thought. The girl could see green eyes, just like her own, a flower with a burning blue colour, and pleasant looking hair that looked ever so fresh indeed. Also, she could tell that the precious life in the distance looked to be made of warm soft butter. Oh, how she dreamed of catching and squeezing the beautiful until a burst of bewitching splendor came all over her body and between her fingers; but of course, acting in such a way would be very uncivil: Harlot had not even yet said hello.

When the beautiful being was no longer in sight, the Ground Faeries crawled out from their places of hiding.

"My goodness, how wonderful," announced the girl to the little women, who were fondling her once again.

"Despicable," hissed a fae who wore a crown made of finch feathers upon her head. "How dare that get in. Those lazy beasts, always neglecting their duties."

"Yak," cried one who wore a crown made of bones.

It happened to be at this time that a gathering of little intrinsically naked beings began to make their way down from the many trees throughout the underground hamlet, while others came from the crystal streams. They were very much like the Ground Faeries, with the additional exception that they had no wings upon their backs and no crowns upon their heads. Also, they seemed a little more delicate and human like in bodily form. (We may call them Wood and Water Nymphs.)

"You're mad!" exclaimed one of the newly arrived beautiful beings. "You didn't hide."

"I am not mad," protested Harlot.

"She is lying," said another Nymph.

"She has to be," said another.

"She always is," said another.

"No I am not," assured the girl, feeling both insulted and overwhelmed by the enticing beings.

"Yes you are," said another.

"I told you," said another.

"She is faking it," said another.

"No I am not," scolded Harlot, much annoyed at the insinuations.

"I do not believe her," said another.

"Me neither," said another.

"I never believed her," said another.

This went on for some time, until every last Nymph had said a statement of their own; some were harsher than others, but in the end they all agreed that the girl was very much mad: she did not act as they did.

Hence the following treatment: the locking up in a forgotten place for three days.

At first there was nothing to keep Harlot's mind busy inside of that dark chamber, but she soon remembered the astonishing sight she had witnessed; this kept her very busy.

Indeed.

By the second day the girl felt quite hungry. Her stomach made strange noises and all she could think about was burnt toast.

For the entirety of the third day Harlot slept.

Once a time had passed, a hatch was lifted over the girl's head, which allowed a warming light to push away the darkness that had been blindingly creeping its way throughout the room. Harlot greeted the Ground Faeries and Wood and Water Nymphs with much hospitality, for she felt well rested, though still hungry; yet, quite use to that feeling, she ignored it.

"We have decided to allow you to join us in our time of carousing," spoke a Nymph who stood in front of the others.

"Yes we have," assured a Faerie who wore a crown made of thorns upon her head.

Oh how the girl loved celebrations, and this was not one to be forgot.

For the past three days all the little women had been working very hard crafting theaters, water slide aqueducts, bouncing ponds of floating mist, little tents for as many as one would like, wood statues and pebble mazes, and everything in between that could possible create a moment of amusement. Though Harlot was a girl of fussy tastes, what now played all around her was indeed as delicious as the finest English Custard.

When the stars of the cave began to grow brighter, as they do at night, the cavern grew darker, and so a towering fire was made within a circle of mushrooms. All of the Ground Faeries and all of the Wood and Water Nymphs gathered inside of the Faerie Ring.

And then it began: There was music. There was dancing. There were many things.

A small fragment of what happened: There was the boisterous fluttering of arms and legs, which followed the very movements of the blazing fire. Though a few of the dancing limbs came close to hitting Harlot on the head and thigh, she managed to escape the blows by caterwauling at those who came near. Yet, as it all looked quite exciting, the girl could not help but join in the gambol, and so went on merrymaking with the others.

(It greaves me to say that I can go no further into the description of this Faerie Ring, as both Faeries and Nymphs are very secretive beings, especially to those they do not know. This small blink will have to do.)

That night, Harlot befriended both a Ground Faerie and a Nymph who seemed to be quite the inseparable pair. Each enjoyed crouching on top of one another, especially on the other's head. The Faerie went by the name of Blue Spek: she wore a crown made of water upon her head and was arguably the prettiest Faerie. As for the Nymph, she went by the name of Pik-Pek: she was just as pretty as her friend, but was also different from the other Nymphs, for she was a half-breed, both Wood and Water Nymph.

Unfortunately, though others would not say so, the evening within the circle came to an abrupt end when the girl lost both of her socks, and one of those socks so happened to fall off her foot inside out. For this reason, she was no longer welcomed by her hostesses and was impolitely banished for the time, as well as her two new friends for similar reasons, out of the underground delight.

Harlot, Blue Spek, and Pik-Pek were thus lead out into the upper-ground along a carpeted tunnel path of moss and downy shrubs. When the three were no longer underground and alone with one another, the light from the stars could no longer be seen; there was a complete darkness.

Since the girl did not enjoy this in the least, she took hold of her friends and ran into no direction in particular, blindly. Even though she could not see the nose upon her face, Harlot could tell that she was running through long, wet, thick, green grass underneath a thicket of tall red trees, and then eventually onto a rougher terrain that felt like path of brown bark.

The girl ran until she could run no more.

Exhausted, she fell asleep.

CHAPTER XIV

ACROSS THE WATER AND UNTO THE SEA

The three-foot-tree, the mog-made-of-scrapes-of-metals-and-woods, and the tortoise where all quite pleased with what they had befallen onto: the dark place was ever so pleasant to be inside.

Eventually, they made their way onto a shore, one covered in fresh clay.

"What in all creations is that?" jarred the mog-made-of-scrapes-of-metals-and-woods, sniffing the frog-thing, which had just fallen from somewhere.

"I do believe it is something like a frog thing," educated the tortoise.

"I have never seen such a strange thing in all my existence," told the exuberated mog-made-of-scrapes-of-metals-and-woods. "Does it always show up uninvited?"

It might have been a delightful acquaintance if the moment had been given a chance; however, the frog-thing spanghewed away. (And that is the last we will ever hear about it.)

At this point, a storm had begun to gather itself together: rains and winds of all sorts. By chance, there was shelter nearby, which laid underneath a grove next to the expired body of a man who appeared to have a can and a head in the same sentence; he was lightly buried under some dung.

While the shelter looked sufficient to give a lifetime of refuge, from cradle to grave, it proved useful for only a short period, for waves of water from the storm quickly tip-toed themselves onto the feet of those harboured within.

Clabang! was one sound that sounded. Kk-k-kkk! was another. It was indeed a sight to see and many a sound to listen to.

With uncertainty, the three pitched themselves a boat: they built its width to an exact measurement of thirty-feet, while its length was argued to be twenty-two feet, and finally its height was to be an estimated fifty-five feet and two quarters. Naturally, a roof was built on the boat, though if it was actually a roof per say was and is much contested: If it was a roof, then both rain and sun could fall into the boat. If there was no roof, then no rain or sun could fall into the boat. (It is a very important discussion worth considering if you have the time.)

Once the boat was finished, the three-foot-tree, the mog-made-of-scrapes-of-metals-and-woods, and the tortoise found there was no need to push themselves into the sea that surrounded them, for the storm had brought it to them.

So off they went into open water with no intent for intent. All three sailed into the sea without planning to plan a purpose. When twenty nights and twenty days had passed, the three-foot-tree broke off a branch from its trunk and dropped it into the water to see if it would float. After several days adrift a decision was made where the three-foot-tree tested the waters with a part of itself. When the branch floated, the three waited a few more days before dropping another branch into the sea. When the time came and the three-foot-tree saw a certain sight, it waited before testing the waters again. On the seventh try the branch no longer floated, for no water flowed underneath the boat. The three-foot-tree eventually saw what it needed to see to know the piece had fulfilled its purpose.

When they had all made their way off of the boat, each had a severe craving for the sight of water. After a long journey, they found themselves another sea and a boat to go with it, and then went adrift into the far distance.

CHAPTER XV

IN A HALLOW

When Harlot awoke, with morning dew on her face, she noticed a plump green worm sitting beside her; it must have come from her fingers, she thought.

"What and who are you?" spoke the unpleasant looking minibeast.

The girl did not like worms in the least, so she swatted the crawling thing with her hand, and then watched it fall, and fall, and fall, until the worm was forgot, for she saw she was lying upon the top of a large dead tree trunk, hanging far above the ground between the branches of two elder trees.

"Oh dear, that is a very long way down," asserted the startled Harlot.

Just then, a small gathering of winged creatures came and sat nearby; they were indeed fascinating things to look at. One could say the newcomers resembled a flock of delicious looking birds, but then one could also say their bodies resembled the likes of knotted vines, the type for soup, fighting for light inside of a chocolate wicker house. There were three creatures in total, and each stood on two long pointed feet and had extraordinarily long stretched wings. Their heads were of the heads of usual birds: two eyes, a beak, little stubs on the side of their heads for ears, and feathers of different shades and colours.

"Would you be able to answer a question of ours?" implored one of the bird creatures, deviously.

"Ask first, then you may have an answer you pestering plagues," scowled Blue Spek, feeling annoyed by the intrusion of space.

"I will," responded a creature in an arrogant tone; then it went on:

They call me a devil.
They call me a rose.
They call me to open.
They call me to close.

The three beings spoke amongst themselves, and then one of them answered, "You would call them stock."

Utterly surprised by the reply, the questioner and its companions noisily chatted to themselves; they believed that whatever had been questioned was much more ignorant. The answer was correct. The things became overtly agitated.

You see, these creatures go by the name of Jaw-Skins. They are the type of creatures that like to ask questions for no intended beneficial reason; the fowls simply squawk matters, but no action or worth is placed in their words, though some may think so.

Thus, after the answer was given, the Jaw-Skins simply went on and on to themselves, excluding all others.

It was during this exchange that Blue Spek and Pik-Pek concluded that it would be a fine time if they were to each jump at a different bird's feet and cling onto it. They did, and the girl thought it silly, so she did the same.

Despite the fun for the others, the creatures were not appreciative; instead, disturbed, they immediately flew off, hoping to somehow detach themselves from the current situation. However, since Harlot had fastened herself so tightly onto the creature's feet, she did not fall off; instead, the bird's body un-weaved from the weight, and down and down she went, twirling all the way. The Faerie and Nymph became much amused by the sight, so they wiggled about until the birds' bodies untangled as well.

In a flurry of hysterics, the Jaw-Skins struck their passengers into one another, striving to detach their nuisances; yet, instead of the intended result, the creatures formed into elflocks, bundling together like beans sprouts in a bowl, ones to certainly cause misfortune in their undoing.

"Shed yourselves you natural fools!" wailed the things together. "Get off! Get off! Get off!"

But of coarse, the girl and her friends did not do so immediately; only when they grew bored did they let go.

And when so, down and down and down they went.

Splish! Splash! Splunk! All three were sunk: They had been consumed by a lusty red liquid.

"My goodness, it is so sweet," announced Harlot, after peeking her tongue onto her wetted lips.

Though the girl, the Faerie, and the Nymph were not aware, they had landed inside of a giant goblet filled with delicious mulberry juice. But such information did not matter to them, for they enjoyed themselves all the same with the splashing game, that is, until it ended when the chalice fell over and spilled its insides out onto the ground.

"I feel so sticky," shouted Harlot, while pressing and pulling her fingers together and apart energetically.

After watching the girl for some time, the beings saw the following: all around were hills and hills of gold things and old things, boxes and obnoxious things, jewelry and diamonds and sapphire and iron; there was something precious for all living and dead things.

"Prikke in a cryk, a nocke in a stok*," declared Pik-Pek, speaking of something currently crawling around in the field of rubbish.

*Literal translation: A jab from a sharp object in a muscle where a spasm is occurring; a groove made at both ends of a tree trunk so to hold a bowstring.

*Symbolic translation: Something unwanted, something useless.

"It's a Nigwig," added Blue Spek.

"Where?" inquired Harlot, trying to spot whatever it was the two where talking about.

"I believe it plans to play a trick on us," replied the Faerie.

"What a despicable creature. A dreadful brute. That is what it is," claimed the girl.

The Nymph toddled in front of Harlot and Blue Spek; she then looked into their direction and uttered the following while waving her arms to add emphases:

"Blanch it in vinegar
Hung in a collar
Lingering past morning sun
With none to pull or holler…"

The rest was not heard, for Pik-Pek began to mumble to herself; there was passion in her speech.

"Wonderful," agreed the Faerie with a smile.

All the while the Nigwig continued to smuggle itself from one place to another, trying not to be seen, which was an unsuccessful effort, for the majority had spotted it quickly enough, and the girl after a time.

Like others of its kind, the Nigwig was a short hairy thing with shaggy garments, which gave ill impression of its actual thin skeletal body. It carried a bludgeon crafted by its own hands made from elder tree sap, known as a Piklure, which it talked to during most occasions. (It is often the voice of the Nigwig that gives away its position, for when such a creature is spotted, it is more often than not seen sitting by the edge of a riverside talking to its bludgeon of plots and wicked plans.)

And so as expected, up around a heap of feathered hats and broken glass, the thing struck up an artifice, which was about to be set in motion: The Nigwig disguised itself.

"Oh my!" sounded the fake, old, helpless woman, after stepping onto Harlot and the others. "I thought you were but a bundle of join stools. Oh bless my eyes. Though grey is the fashionable colour."

"We are not," retorted the Faerie, annoyed, to say a degree of the least.

"Yes this is true," replied the old, helpless woman. "But please forgive my fading sight, for it strays me more and more as the days go by. I am a real old woman in need." The old women then took something out from her pocket, which was in the shape of a handkerchief, and swung it in circles while singing with an awful pitch:

"Phrivorlous phrompulis phimpulus pho,
Tell me now!
Toodidel-do.
If not, I shall beat you
On your head and your toes,
My walking stick shall smite
Until your skin starts to grow."

"I do not know what you are talking about you marble headed goat," attacked Harlot, infuriated by the idea that the creature meant to play a trick on her.

"Why be so cruel to those who pass your own years?" inquired the woman. "We may upset you with prospects of your own comings, but do be kind and spare me something to eat. So long have I travelled and am in need of your in-dwindle heart."

The Nigwig then made the presence of its Piklure known, which had a cloth attached to it in the shape of a begging pot. As this allowed for a closer engagement, it began to poke around with something else in an ill-intending manner.

There was a silent agreement that then took place between the girl, the Faerie, and the Nymph: They dug a pit and put the thing in it. When the dirt was put back in place, they smoothed out the ground, for it looked pretty to look at when the sun touched it.

CHAPTER XVI

OUTSIDE THE HOLLOW

The night came onto them, as well as the night after that. They eventually took up the pacing of feet during the time of day and journeyed onto the outskirts of a large pointed fence.

Inside the fence were bodies doing work that seemed to prevail to no purpose: Some were cutting off branches of trees, only to try to sew them back on with broken string a few moments later. Others were throwing stones into the air, then tapped them three times with a wilted flower once they hit the ground.

A loud shout was made, and then some bodies were put into a straight line, numbered, used, and then discarded.

Harlot looked through the fence at the bodies within until a man in bitten skin stuck himself in front of her, standing with high held feet.

He shouted the following between his closed teeth: "Where are you going during this hour and why are you on that side of the fence?"

"I have no desire to become a hat for a headless man," told the girl.

The man was so angered by Harlot's response, he leisurely picked up a twig that laid underneath some dirt, spit on it, then threw it through the fence into the girl's face, then spat on the ground three times. But then an assortment of bells began to chant from within the fenced area, so the man took off in a hurry, smiling as went; it was as if he was about to give a ladle of soup from the very top of a pot to some starving bodies. He then disappeared into a mascaraed of others who looked exactly like him.

"I would certainly not enjoy myself if I was to go on the other side of that fence," assured the girl.

And so onto another other place they went.

CHAPTER XVII

ONTO ANOTHER PATH; OF A LAKE OF LADIES

As Harlot walked, she did not enjoy the time in the least: The path was filled with sneaky scattered stones constantly growing out from the ground, unapologetically performing their cunning arts of tasteless trickery. Suddenly, they would appear, again and again, pleased to place themselves in front of her feet, trying to trip her, in both body and thought. Oh how the girl despised stumbling over them; they were all just a terrible nuisance. Yet, as time went on, she began to get a little more cunning herself. Whenever one of the distresses was spotted, Harlot kicked about as hard as she could, causing much around to scatter off into the distance; she very much enjoyed watching the pieces of rock run from her feet, away and away, no longer there to cause her to stagger and fall.

On one similar occasion, after sending her foot forth to meet with a stone that had figured out a way to make her tumble, the girl sent it tip-tapping, inadvertently leading towards a place that was of something to be seen, but most often not to be believed. Not too far over to the right and then a little to the left at the top of a mound, next to the newly struck concretion, was a tree.

Harlot's eyes gawk at the sight they saw.

The tree stood standing on the elevation, its branches sprawled in every direction, while its leaves were quite different to the ones one would usually expect (but there is no need to describe their resemblance to sugar feathers, for underneath is what is worth sketching in words).

Down below, where the shadings met hand in hand, dripped the drippiest droplets one could have ever thought to grasp.

It was raining underneath the tree.

While some of the droplets bore an undimmed luster inside, from far away the glows of the water drops could only be distinguished as a mere blunting haze; yet, if one were to get close enough, if they dared admit or do the such, the privated brightness that laid inside could be seen each as uniqueness, every and each in their very own way.

"Oh how marvelous!" exclaimed the girl.

"It is The Cuckut-Tree of The Garden Ladies," explained Blue Spek, with eyes on her face that did not match Harlot's.

"Why is the tree dripping? If I were to go below to try to get some shade, I would most definitely be wetted in every place possible," questioned and then told the girl.

"Agreed," chuckled the Ground Faerie, not taking the matter seriously. "In any event, the tree drips a droplet every time a blue rose is eaten, and the glowing droplets only drip when a blue rose is blown upon."

Harlot's eyes spread open even wider with all the talk of blue things.

"I want to eat a blue rose or blow on one so that I could watch a droplet drip because of me," told the girl.

"I believe yours has already fallen," told Blue Spek.

And sure enough, when Harlot looked closer, she saw a luster that was her own, but it had not fallen because of her own will. The girl's glow, as well as more than many others, were all forcefully submerged into the pond that lay underneath the tree.

"I feel as if though I would very much enjoy getting any part of myself wet. The water looks so lovely. I do believe I will touch it. I will touch it," informed Harlot, not understanding why she felt that way.

The girl ignorantly made both her feet bare and bent herself down towards the water. Yet, before she was close enough to slip her fingers into the wetness, she was placed aback by three beguiling beings who emerged from underneath, now pointing their faces in her direction.

"It is the Cuckut-Ladies," introduced Blue Spek. "They are to stay within these waters, while others somewhere else."

Harlot met their bodies with her eyes and observed, "They are so pretty to look at."

The three beings were each tucked away from their middles down. When the girl made herself closer, she could see that that their bottom halves were adorned with ruff purple pearls, and each, instead of two, seemed to only have one foot at the base of their bodies, ones as wide as the opening between the girl's own stretched legs and feet, measured from toe-tip to toe-tip. (With closer observation, Harlot would have noticed that the feet were not actually feet, but instead large fins.) Only a scant of the lower halves could sometimes be caught in sight however, for those parts were closeted by the brightness of the underwater droplets. Yet, the top halves were not as niggardly. The girl watched as the droplets dripped from the branches of the tree, down onto the ladies' hair and white shoulders; those holding a glow within lit up all around wherever they went, slowly rolling down onto the beings' front or backsides, meeting with the water of the pond below.

The three finned ladies each took part in the following lyrical melody, while stuck underneath the tree:

The seafaring folk
Come cracking their shackles,
Their anchors, their tackles,
Reeling with hooks.

'Come smell the poppies,'
They call, they call.
'Come smell the poppies.
Come all, come all.'

First taken and shaken
N'walloped about.
But oh, the poppies.
We need more poppies!

So they sprinkle their babies
Then blow on the ladies,
Sipping the broth
Straight from the bowl!

'Back to the Poppy-House,'
They call, they call.
'Back to the Poppy-House.

Come all, come all'

With eyes staying sighted,
All are invited,
Singing the songs,
Which they had all brew.

'Come smell the poppies,'
They call, they call.
'Come smell the poppies.
Come all, come all.'

As the ladies finished singing their ignored song, a respectable looking man in a black suit, who was of good breed and filled with dapperness, made his way towards Harlot with a small book in his hand.

"What a pretty looking thing," spoke the man-in-the-black-suit to the little girl. He looked her up and down, all the while writing in his book; when finished, he continued. "Do you enjoy raw poppy pies?"

"I do not believe I have ever tasted such a thing. However, I would enjoy some Maple-Milk. Do you have any?" inquired Harlot, feeling awfully thirsty for something sweet.

"Here you are," replied the man-in-the-black-suit, as he handed the girl a morsel of a raw poppy pie, which was cut into slithers so that the poopy juices seeped out.

"That looks like stones. I despise stones. Where is my Maple-Milk?" inquired Harlot with much frustration.

"Eat some pie first, pretty girl," insisted the thing. "Only after you eat every last seed will you get your drink."

Harlot wanted Maple-Milk, but not to this degree; thus, she would have never touched the seeds if the man had not taken a handful and stuffed them right into her mouth, bulging her cheeks beyond what she could stand. At first, the seeds squirmed around like rotten cheese, crawling around her mouth in tender maggoty movements, but eventually she began to very much enjoy the funny feelings, for there was a reward to be had after the transgression.

Before the man went on his way, he gave the three water women half-raw poppy pies, both to please and keep bound. Once the beings gobbled them up, to the very seed, they took the girl's hands and pressed their lips upon them. They then did the same to both her feet. Harlot enjoyed this so very much that her body fell into the water and she was then among Cuckut-Ladies.

Blue Spek and Pik-Pek slipped in too.

The clocks ticked and toked, and the sun and the moon trudged through nights and days.

The following was the girl's entry:

Mrs. Harlot, Under the Cuckut-
Tree

> *This youthful ruby lays as if slain*
> *before and after, even if little sweets*
> *are brought for cheering. Her teeth*
> *are very clean and fair, as well as the*
> *girl's blessed eyes, which on her face*
> *are very large and green. If searching*
> *for circles of the fledging type—*
> *though   costly—this   un-farrowing*

damsel is very well suited for fumbling keepers. On account of a good piece, she does not keep coin herself; one must place a brace of shiners into the red hat before introducing the blind visitor—or even prior to any type of dealing for that matter. Make sure the hedges are thick, for the squawks are rich.

One evening, Harlot saw the moon through the sky when she looked up. At first it was grey, but then it turned red and bubbled like a bowl of boiling porridge. She tried to pull herself out of the warm water, but she was pulled aback into the garden of poppies that sprung all around; her fingers began to feel like sticky candied webs full of things that fell all around the clouds. Her toes felt the same. She could see herself and the stars all at once, but could never really understand where she had gone.

"The sounds never make themselves through the walls," remarked the girl, after she had fortunately been put back into the water for the last time.

It was at this occasion, both Blue Spek and Pik-Pek, though they were too afraid to bring their thoughts forward before, not only because of an inevitable carting, but also because there are only deaf ears willing to listen to such types of things, managed to escape, which is a practically unrealistic situation.

When no one was looking, they forced Harlot from the water and flung her to the very top of a distant tree. The girl protested the event, but was pressed on to stay until her friends allowed her to come down.

After a time, Harlot found a hole in one of the branches, which she cuddled into. Some nights the girl stayed up in the tree, shaking from the cold; she would hold her arms around her legs so tightly that several times they almost fell off. Though on those days she never tried to climb down. On others, Harlot attempted to sneak her way past the guarding eyes of the Faerie and Nymph, but to no avail on her side; she was placed back at the very top where she stayed for many a night and day.

Eventually, Blue Spek and Pik-Pek aided the girl safely down. Once on the ground, Harlot ran off and away from the direction of the tree until her legs could run no more. After she rested for a few moments, she stood up and ran some more.

CHAPTER XVIII

A BAND OF EUNUCHS WITH ONION SACS ON THEIR HEADS

As Harlot ran, she stared at her feet. The girl did not care where they took her, as long as it was away from where she had been.

One day, she fell off the edge of a precipice.

Down, down, down, she went.

Blue Spek and Pik-Pek watched, then discussed, then placed themselves by Harlot's side, then sewed tasty mushrooms onto her fingertips, cheeks, and thighs; all the while, the girl continued to fall down, down, down.

The happenings made Harlot squirm, not because of the needles and threads, but because the remaining poppy seeds began to seep out and away from her body in ever an awful manner. The girl grasped with her fingers, desperately trying to snatch at the black beads as they made themselves away, but she could not catch even one.

When purged, she hit the ground.

Harlot moved her dress and herself about for inspection; she unveiled that instead of her own limbs, it was the mushrooms that were no longer attached to her body. They were all squished and about, like drips of jam ready for biscuits. In a way, she was pleased about the outcome, though the stitches, which remained upon her, made it all quite itchy.

Nevertheless, a sight quickly shifted the girl's attention: A vast field covered in onion vines, all nicely placed in scattered bunches, laid in front of her.

Pik-Pek picked up an onion and began to eat it.

Thinking well of the idea, Harlot plucked an assortment of onions, filling her plackets until no more could be fit; she was quite hungry. But before the girl could begin to eat her harvest, a large group of eunuchs had surrounded her on every side.

The eunuchs were of about Harlot's size, each dressed in their best Sunday clothes. On their heads were onion sacs decorated with two holes for their eyes and one hole for their mouth.

The girl noticed that the onion sacs were sewed to their faces with a different coloured string than the one she had all over her body; while her stitches were dark purple, theirs were another colour, a pumpkin like colour. She wondered if they too had fallen off the edge of a cliff and hit the ground in the same fashion.

During Harlot's time of pondering, the eunuchs stood completely still; that is, until one of them cried out in a pleasant high-pitched voice, "We must check to see if she is one of us."

And so they checked.

And so she was.

When satisfied with what they saw, the eunuchs presented themselves to the girl and her friends and then sang the following ballad in choir with the most elegant of voices:

Always be kind to a farmer's wife,
For in his barn lays a jagged knife.
He'll cut you up and lay you down,
Upon the fields and upon the ground.

Things will sprout from your scattered body,
Prospering from your corpse that's rotting.
The sun will come out and shine each day;
The birds will feast and shout Hurray!

And for years and years things will grow,
Through rain storms, hail, and even snow.
Then up and up you'll sprout a toadstool,
Soon to fall, crying no one told you!

So if you see a farmer's wife,
Always be kind and act real nice.

Harlot could not help but clap at the wonderful sounds, both during, before, and after the singing. Some of the eunuchs took bows, while others curtsied. It was indeed a merry moment for them all.

As the eunuchs began to make aesthetically pleasing noises of harmony once more, the girl became so excited at the following sight that she began to jump up and down: A flock of unshorn lambs were stampeding into her direction.

"Lambs! Lambs! Lambs!" ejaculated Harlot.

And lambs surrounded them all on every side.

The girl continued to bounce about, shouting, making sure that all heard: "Oh how I adore lambs. They are so funny to look at."

"Do you want to ride one?" asked a eunuch who was tired of listening to Harlot's interruptions, for she had been loudly expressing herself while they had been singing.

Curiously, the girl's eyes opened wide, moistened, and her body became still. All the eunuchs stared at her for several moments, wondering if she had suddenly fallen ill, soon to be scattered onto a field for things to grow from.

However, little did the onlookers know, before and during this anxious situation, Blue Spek and Pik-Pek had entered Harlot's placket and had been enjoying her onions. And, when the two had finished eating up the layered delicacies, they decided to grabble around inside, pushing about the crackly onionskins to see if there were any delicious bulbs left. Because of this, the Faerie accidentally, or perhaps not, for Faeries do have the gift of multiplying, pinched the girl. When this happened, Harlot's eyes opened wide, moistened, and her body became still. Then she ran over to one of the lambs, jumped on its back, and rode off with great speed.

How exciting it all was, and the girl very much enjoyed every moment of it.

This is what happened:

She rode away from the eunuchs, past the onion vines, past watching eyes, and into a glass valley, where the grass glimmered like salty ice-sticks, and the sun tickled like sour powder. On and on Harlot went, feeling herself within her skin as a warm wind passed between her body.

Alas, when the time came, the girl saw in front of her a woman, more beautiful than can be described, but will be anyways: This woman had hair; but instead of the most beautiful brown one could ever imagine, her hair was completely white, like that of pasty cotton, freshly picked to be placed into a longing bowl of rice pudding. This woman had a face; but instead of that of unblemished youth, her face was a bit more seasoned, though still very much within her bloom. This woman had a gown that covered her body; but instead of that of a girl, the gown was that of a woman. And, if one followed her from the top of her frock down to the bottom, one would notice that at the end, those delicate limbs, the one's often spoken highly about but never in earnest, were not visible; instead, below flowed a boat made of clouds, swaying in a riverbed of mist.

The lady, in a simple word, was a Faedress, a beautiful being that held both skin and clothes in the most elegant of fashions, destined to spend eternity rowing through the skies, watching below.

Sadly, the meeting only lasted for two moments; indeed it was not as long as forever. But during this time, Harlot joined the woman in the clouds on many sights and sounds through plights inbound for places in particular.

Then, as rain eventually comes, the girl dripped with the droplets back onto the lamb she had ridden; it brought her to the other sheep and eunuchs, who all watched Harlot's return.

"Are you a damsel of the trees?" questioned one of the eunuchs.

The girl was not in the mood for answering questions, so she did not answer. With her eyes wide open, she wondered if she herself could ride on the brink of a boat and sail herself from the shadows behind to the fading light that somehow lay ahead in the distance.

Harlot then sang a song (though the words have been lost).

All of the eunuchs listened.

When finished, one of the eunuchs tapped the girl's shoulder and asked, "Are you a damsel of the trees?"

Harlot did not reply.

"If so," the eunuch continued, "please accept these words of mine."

And the eunuch offered her kind words, and she accepted them.

The girl bid the eunuch thanks with her mouth, "Thank you."

After speaking, though untimely, Harlot's face began to blush: A sudden urge to pluck some flowers had come over her. While in great desperation to find a more private place, she squeezed her thighs together as tightly as she could, bouncing about, until a nice looking area presented itself, and so went to meet with it.

When finished, a little dampened from her doings, the threads upon the girl's body began to fidget and twist, and then let out an assortment of dark coloured roses. This event did not bother Harlot in the least, nor did it frighten her, though she was a little glum that no blue roses had come out.

She danced about in a delightful manner, reciting, "La la la…la la la…la la la—"

Then she tripped over something and fell into a hole.

CHAPTER XIX

A TOWER

When the girl opened her eyes, she noticed that she was lying on her head, back, bottom, and feet at the end of a deep tunnel, one that led nowhere.

"My goodness, I feel like the Old Tailor," announced Harlot.

The Tale of the Old Tailor

There sat an Old Tailor three times too old,
Waiting for fancies to tear up their hold.
But in vain he would sit he would sit he would sit,
Sipping the lead until he lost his wit.

And to join himself in these midmorning brews,
He had a pewter plate with tomatoes undue.
Lushes and scrumptious and blubbery about,
Each finely filed, covered with a clout.

But there came the day when the sun went away,
And there came the knell that sounded and swayed.
So out came the table and no laded ruck,
And out came the ladle with no mouths to suck.

To make sure of fate, he sat on the table,
But soon he was seated in an arable.
They awaited the string to see if it slacked,
But never it sounded, so they turned their backs.

Nevertheless, though the girl was not the Old Tailor, she too was unable to raise herself up from where she laid.

It was the fault of the roses: so many had grown from her body, restricting her movement, while also crawling up the sides of the hole, attaching themselves onto whatever they could grasp, searching, and then finding the sunlight that made itself above.

Yet, for Harlot below, with great exertion, and with the help of the Faerie and Nymph, she tore the roots of the flowers out from deep within the stitches, and in due course was able to move again.

"My skin feels quite smooth. Very smooth. I thought it would all be ruff," informed the girl, as she touched herself.

Blue Spek and Pik-Pek giggled.

"What are you laughing at? Tell me. I find it very troublesome that you have not told me what seems to be a very comical something," questioned and then demanded Harlot.

The Faerie whispered into the girl's ear, and then she too joined in.

It was all quite amusing.

Once finished, and placing reflections upon their present situation, the beings began the building of a tall vertical structure, starting from the bottom of the hole, aiming towards an upwards direction; the plan was to make themselves to the level of the ground, and then a little further.

A stone went there, then another there, then another other, until after a long and tiresome work, the beings managed to thrust forth a fully functional tower. Yet, once the last stone was put into its proper place, the girl realized that they had trapped themselves within the new walls, a type that went towards the sky instead of away from it: They had forgotten to fabricate a door. With deep distress, all pressed themselves back towards the downwards direction.

Many silent and still eves passed, until one nightfall came, a time when the three within the ground heard lovely sounds coming from far above their heads. Harlot was the first, though closely followed by Blue Spek and Pik-Pek, to begin to walk up the tower steps to look for what they heard.

When the girl arrived, she squealed in eager delight, while her eyes gapped wide, taking in every sight they could see.

In front, were several charming somethings wearing un-torn masks upon their faces, all of which were rather intriguing to the senses. Each had limbs that could fit into a vanilla-jar with ease, and eyes that would fill a honey-pale to the brim. Many trawled for Harlot's attention by joining one another in perfectly rounded circles, some wide and others clenched, singing sounds of merry.

The somethings frolicked around, moving in every way and direction, until a shower of colourful powders came pouring out from beneath their masks, covering the somethings and the ground around them, like spilt bowls of the most exotic of spices.

After a moment of rest, the somethings took hold of the girl's dress, and then spun her around in circles. Harlot enjoyed herself very much, especially when her feet lifted off of the ground from all of the excitement.

When the event reached its peak, the girl was thrown against the tower wall until she broke through.

And so out she went, tumbling first into the air, and then down onto a dewy grass below, followed by the Faerie and the Nymph. As Harlot stood on her knees, she could feel a rush come over her. With happiness, she kissed Blue Spek and Pik-Pek upon their faces, and then laid herself down and took time for rest.

"I feel as if my heart has moved through my mouth and feet and fingers," told the girl afterwards, as she stretched her limbs.

Then there was a gasp.

The others gasped as well.

Upon the ground laid a little being, worn. She had no colour, no eyes, no flower, was seen by many as no longer buttery, and was forced to lay where anyone could know her freely, as she could no longer fly.

"I know what that is. Oh how beautiful. How wonderful. That is a Butter-Maiden," declared Harlot.

And so the girl took the being and held her close; the Butter-Maiden did the same.

But of coarse, there was to be the inevitable carting.

End of Volume I

Volume II

CHAPTER I

THE GIRL AND THE CART

After the night passed away, Harlot took the hand of the Butter-Maiden and helped the little being off of the ground. Her name was Lady. She had a pretty face and pretty fingers, each embraced with white rings made of lead, which she used to scratch her head with whenever she got itchy, and other such useful purposes, like scratching away at trees to suck out their sap. Also, upon the Butter-Maiden's toes were little pieces of cloth to keep her warm.

Indeed she was a pretty being all throughout.

The girl and Lady enjoyed one another's company very much; they seemed to always be in the midst of merry doings with one another. The Faerie and Nymph took a liking to the Butter-Maiden as well, even though their kinds are not known for such behaviour in each-others' presence.

In commemoration of the joyful times, they all inscribed their pleasures in a bounded book, one that held a carving of a hole on the cover, which came to be filled with both wondrous pictures and pleasant words. All four could have made many more books about each other and what they did together, but only one was made, which was kept tied to Harlot's thigh, for practical purposes.

One of the entries follows:

To make a Dashely Dumely Cake…

Take four handfuls of flowers, roughly mingled with a gathering of honey. Add them into a bucket full of warmed milk. Boil for a few moments before adding in more honey and fingers full of sweet dough. Cook at a reasonable temperature until a warm cake is formed.

Then, as such things come to be, a time eventually came when the book was buried.

And, soon after the event, when the girl and the others were standing next to a pale of parch looking water, a gathering of humble looking creatures dawdled by. The things looked exceptionally virtuous: behind their heads glowed empty moons, which floated with the help of both of each's hands.

"Where do you believe they are going?" asked one of the beings to her companions.

"I think they're making their way to a mountain top so that they can get close enough to a cloud for touching," responded another being.

In reaction to the words, Harlot fell to her bottom and thought of the following: She imagined herself within the presence of a gathering of clouds, all pressing themselves around her with raindrops and softness. She could fancy herself spinning and spinning with her dress pushing out onto all sides, spinning until all the clouds turned into rain, then falling with them; and when the time came, she would rise with the clouds once more.

But the girl's jaunty thoughts were soon brought to an end, for from another direction approached a cart made of wrought iron. Within it laid a tree, but instead of growing with unbroken branches, it grew with broken ones; and on the outside were several hooded and hunched figures, all with drippings falling from between vain lines upon their backs. They pulled the cart through the use of ropes, ones that fitted nicely through a hole in each of their hands, a delightful stigma per say, subsequently keeping the openings perpetually moist to imitate earthly mortification.

After the dripping-figures stopped before the beings and brought about a few more openings on their own backs with the aid of a thin string, they enthusiastically used kneaded ropes to capture Harlot, Blue Spek, Pik-Pek, and Lady, then were put into the cart.

"Salvay!" proclaimed all but the prisoners, even the creatures who held empty moons behind their heads, whom of which then began to sing the following tune as they walked into a distance; they had the same intentions as the dripping-figures, but in another place:

Oh-ummm…
Oh-ummm…
Oh…
Off to the bakers to bake us a pie
(Off to the bakers to bake us a pie)
And dawdle our tongues until their turn to rye
(And dawdle our tongues until their turn to rye)
Up to the mountains
(Up to the mountains)
Up to the mountains to frolic our rings
Up to the mountains to pander our kings
Oh-ummm…
Oh-ummm…
Oh-ummm…

So long was the path of the cart.

After brought through many towns, all of which scorned its occupants and hissed things they themselves hid behind their own curtains, the dripping-figures placed the cart and its occupants in a fenced clearing within a woodland.

As a certain daylight went away, the girl and the others were pushed out of the cart and onto the ground, with the addition of the cutting off of the Faerie's wings: an exploit made to deter escape by flight. The dripping-figures took the dismembered leaves, cooked them in a bucket full of flames, and then ate the ashes.

The night was also planed by the things to be one of fulfilling intensions; however, though Blue Spek was partly devastated by the loss of her wings, for she could always put on another pair, she came up with a plan of escape.

The beings dug a hole underneath a part of the fence, which they all then tried to creep under. Unfortunately, one of the dripping-figures noticed the happening; so it placed another fence around the failed escapers, which went both over and under ground.

"This is just terrible, just terrible," announced the girl.

The Butter-Maiden held Harlot tight.

As the evening continued to grow black and even more despairing, the dripping-figures made more drips fall from their backs, as this was part of the preparation for their particular subjugation, a prepaid penance per say, then surrounded their prisoners on all sides, hissed and howled, laughed and prowled, and then leaped in at their prey.

But by well chance (though it might seem like coincidence, it is not), the spit of Blue Spek made itself into the eyes of the savages and so blinded them physically, forever.

Because of this, the girl and her friends were able to make themselves away from their entrapments and the horrid place, which caged those who remained within until they shriveled up and died.

CHAPTER II

TOGETHER TOWARDS A HOUSE UPON A MOUNTAIN

At a certain moment, a single want troubled Harlot's head: she wished to touch a cloud, just as the Faerie had deduced to be the intensions of the empty moon creatures, which seemed to be many a long time ago. So off the beings went towards a mountain, towards the clouds.

A situation: Though the girl wished to take a path that led straight up the mountain, for that was the quickest way to her destination, one which she very much wanted to get to as fast as possible, the Faerie protested at the idea. (You see, during this occasion of a delicate deliberation, one that had to do with the girl's desire, Blue Spek found a pair of wings on the back of a bird who no longer had any use of them; taking an immediate liking, she sowed and sewed the wings onto her own back: beautiful indeed. For this reason, the Faerie did not want to go directly up the mountain.) So they went around while slowly moving in an upward direction.

And many nights and days were spent travelling from one side to the next; fortunately (for us all), interesting happenings were found upon the way.

At one place, within some grass, there laid little stones, but not the kind that Harlot had met so often before; these were of a different sort: they were the type that made the most peculiar of humming noises and were quite conscientious and polite to those who happened to be stepping by.

At one point, the girl picked up a few of said stones and was asked a riddle, each thing sounding a single word one after another:

What do you see
When you do not see me
When you climb a tree
And enter with glee

Harlot thought and thought. Then she stopped. Then started again. Then stopped again. Then started one last time before she stopped again: She continued to have an absentminded and a much too trusting contemplation. The stones hummed some more then made themselves onto the ground and away.

There was also another exciting event that took place; this fancy caught both the girl's eyes and fingers: Between several trees that grew ever so close to one another, were little pockets of wetness. When Harlot first spotted the tree-puddles, she observed blankets of little bubbles coming out from within them; and so she told the others. This caused a great degree of excitement for all of the witnesses, especially Lady who believed it to be tree sap.

The girl animatedly stuck her fingers right in-between the long limbs of one of the coupled trees.

"Oh my! It feels so warm and slippery around my finger tips," exclaimed and then told Harlot, also feeling a softness;

she motioned the others to come and put their fingers into the pockets of wetness as well.

It was a wonderful collaborative sight to see and be in as the beings dipped their fingers into the tree puddles, and sometimes poked at one another's eyes, as the such was what they wanted to do. In particular, the Butter-Maiden very much enjoyed herself, indulging in as much as she possibly could. Yet, in consequence for all, their fingers, and Lady's mouth, began to let out blankets of bubbles of their own.

"I wonder what the bubbles taste like?" wondered the girl.

At the thought of the idea, Harlot put all of her fingers straight into her mouth, all at once, then took them out, then put them close, then back in, and then back out again, letting some wetness drip from her mouth and fingers onto the ground. After a while of this, she realized that it would be much more exciting to catch the bubbles coming out from the Butter-Maiden's mouth rather than the ones coming from herself; so with the help of Lady's lips, the girl filled and filled and filled her own with so many bubbles, soon to be joined with the enjoyment and giggles and tasting of the others.

CHAPTER III

Not long after, the beings reached the mountaintop. The place looked to be a very pleasant place, where all could go and enjoy themselves in goodwill; there were birds singing upon leaves and branches and flowers, while a delicious smell crept itself throughout the air, like fresh pies straight from a baker's oven. However, a house had been constructed upon an attractive mound on the mountaintop. The building was neither large nor spacious, but there was no mistaking its obvious existence, though denials could be made that it was of some other place entirely. Blinds covered more windows than not, white satin keeping the tenants subdued; torches lit the entrance way, red pieces to call out to proud patrons; and cross bones for those to be denied dignity now and after, green decaying cloth stewing about to be trampled upon by all.

It looked to be a pleasant place with all its colours.

Nevertheless, what groped Harlot and the others in was a forever spinning Water-Drop ring laying upon the knob of a door; the delectable looking item appeared to be waiting for someone to devour it all in a moments notice. Yet, none of the beings were able to have a taste, for a man had viciously opened the door, made himself behind the girl, forced himself inside, pushing Harlot through the doorway, and then left to somewhere else verily chanting as pleased as could be.

As a numbness took over, the girl continue on; she went further into the house, seeing many pretty beings, all of which were damsels dressed in silken green garments. Few had pretty blue roses upon themselves, for most had other coloured ones, which were scattered there and about upon their bodies. Some of the damsels stood upon one another, some dangled on each other's shoulders, some sang songs, and some sat perfectly still.

Eyeing more within the house, Harlot came to see many creatures as well; they called themselves the Gently Gentlemen. Each looked different, but all were the same within. Some wore smocks, others wore hats, some wore things upon their feet, others wore things upon their hands. However, all held cocksure grimaces upon their faces, or hidden, ready to take all the pretty boxes and pleasing cases they could find, 'trull-la-la-ing' all the way along, for sure enough it was empty tokens that weighed plackets down, for that was the law of the house.

"Oh how pretty," remarked the girl, for something else caught her fancy.

It was a little book containing both writings and pictures of pretty women, many of which were in that very room. Harlot gasped and marveled at the many drawings, flipping one page, and then another, and then another other page, giggling the entire time, until one of the Gently Gentlemen took the book from her; he had attained some heavy tokens from a wager and wanted to make use of them.

Though the girl was annoyed at the nasty beast, her emotions did not develop further, for she saw several of the

creatures that held empty moons behind their heads walking
about the house. Harlot decided to make herself to the front
of one in particular; he had the longest string that hung
from his waist, which even touched the ground. She thought
it quite silly.

The girl readily commented on and then asked the man
politely, for she wished to please such a virtuous looking
thing, "Your string will get dirty hanging so low. How do
you do?"

"Oh how the clouds will shine upon me this evening,"
rejoiced the empty-moon-creature with a growing smile, as
he placed a trinity of eyes towards Harlot. "Would you care
to accompany me to the top of the house?"

"Yes indeed. That is a wonderful suggestion,"
respectively replied the girl, excited by the mentioning of
clouds.

And so up to the top of the house the two climbed, first
putting their feet on wood steps, and then brick, eventually
making themselves up to the top of the house where there
hung elegantly treated hollow logs upon the walls. The man
tossed a few tokens into one of them; a door was forced
wide open, revealing a dark narrow room.

They both went inside.

"Oh how quaint," voiced Harlot, as she noticed thick
carpets stuck upon the walls, each holding patterns of funny
things to look at.

When they were both completely within the room, the
door quickly shut and the virtuous-looking-thing shouted
with all his might, as if in an immense amount of pain; he
then stood still and quite, prying his ear about. The girl
became irritated by the unpleasant outburst of shouting, so

she looked out a bare window, one very thick with glass, and happened to spot a cloud that laid not too far from her fingers.

"What are you doing little girl?" asked the empty-moon-creature with curiosity.

Harlot looked at the man, perplexed at his supposed ignorance of the not too distant cloud outside, and then proclaimed as she spun in circles, "I believe a cloud is making itself ready this evening. I just know it will drip about if it is touched. Just look at it. It is so wonderful."

The virtuous-looking-thing was surprised by the girl's agreeable response, and so continued to enquire, "Is there anything that would further facilitate you little girl?"

"I wish to touch a cloud of coarse," told Harlot.

"A cloud!" shouted the empty-moon-creature. "You cannot touch a cloud. How despicable. Only I may touch a cloud."

"No! No! No! I can touch a cloud. I have before. Well, to some degree. But that is of no importance. Oh how wonderful they are. I wish I could touch all of their soft looking delicateness. If only my fingers were long enough to spread themselves out and reach their softness, deep inside. Oh how I wish to stroke them, for they seem so pleasant," shouted, asserted, and then fantasized the girl.

But to Harlot's displeasure, the cloud she looked upon did not make its way towards her. She was not able to hold onto it and squeezed it tight within her fingers, feeling its softness, making it spurt out dripplets of water, turning it into puddles of wetness. Instead, at the very same moment the cloud drifted away, the man took the girl away from the window and smiled at her with his teeth.

The virtuous-looking-thing then urged the following: "Come now, do not keep the clouds hidden this evening."

Harlot once again became irritated, as it was quite obvious that the cloud outside was now gone. The girl demanded and then protested for the door of the room to be opened so she could make herself away from the place, but the empty-moon-creature approached her in a frightening manner and caught her by the dress.

"Stop your imprudence and quit looking glower," bawled the empty-moon-creature into Harlot's face. "Are you honest girl? Tell me now."

Harlot, outraged that her honesty had been questioned, screamed out, "How dare you! I am no liar!"

The girl could no longer endure the presence of the man; she attempted escape, but found no way out.

"Ha," laughed the virtuous-looking-thing. "You are stuck here until I know you well. But not here; it is no longer sufficient for what I have in mind. I will take you some place else."

And so the empty-moon-creature went on his way, lugging Harlot to a fountain that lay not too far from the house on the mountain; all the while the girl wondered how she could allow the man to know her well enough to be satisfied with the existence of her honesty. In any event, when they arrived, the virtuous-looking-thing placed Harlot next to the fountain, trying to make her wet. Yet, he soon tripped over a well-placed rock and thus fell into the fountain water. Splashes and ripples he did make, and soon enough fell deeper and deeper underneath the water's edge below.

The girl looked on with partial justice, for the witnessed event was much less than deserved. Un-coincidentally, Blue Spek, Pik-Pek, and Lady all came out from underneath the very same place the empty-moon-creature had gone down. They embraced Harlot, thankful they had found her not a moment later.

As it was quite late, they all made themselves underneath a tree for the evening. They watched with warming fingers and faces as the house on the mound on the mountain, and all but for the beings within, were turned into a pile of flames, ridding the place of all those who were the same within.

It was a pleasing sight.

Thus, they put their heads down and fell asleep.

CHAPTER IV

MANY OCCURRENCES WHILE GETTING TO THE HOUSE OF HOSPITALITY

All would have slept much longer than they did if it were not for the noise of a nuisance: a dastardly crow.

"What a horrid way to live," grumbled the Faerie.

The Nymph agreed with a nod, then whispered the following to those close by:

> "If I had a pocket,
> One full of pebbles,
> I would throw it just far enough
> To make it fall like fettles."

But for ill chance, a crow-keeper, who was entirely covered in bark and false tree sap, came stalking by. At seeing the beings, and hearing the sounds of the crow, the man was quick to react, hoping that the situation was of the opportunistic sort; and so he lifted one of his legs into the air and made some awful noises, noises that made the sounds of the crow seem delicate and delightful to listen to.

The following was what the crow-keeper cried out: "Whak-k wak waka! Yy-ah errr. Yy-ah errr aaa!" (And so on.)

Although the crow continued to squawk, the man approached the Butter-Maiden, expecting to be rewarded. Since the crow-keeper was covered in what seemed to be so much tree sap, yet a small amount would have made no difference, Lady became lock-headed, licking her lips with thoughts of scratching away at the bark and sucking out every bit of its sap.

Yet, the girl was very much angered by the man and his meaning to her friend; so she kicked him as hard as her foot would let her. In response, the crow-keeper shouted some more (I will not repeat his sounds, for they are much too irritating).

After more kicking, Harlot managed to repel the haughty creature, who eventually fell down a crag and broke his neck.

Following the soothing of the girl's aching foot, which comprised of the delicate rubbings with many relieving herbs, preformed by Blue Spek and Pik-Pek, but not the Butter-Maiden, for she continued to be upset about the tree sap for awhile longer, they continued on.

"My goodness. What is that over there?" wondered Harlot.

All waited to see what the girl could have seen. Alas, it was no Kelpie, but a mare, and it immediately galloped up to their faces.

"How gross. Your spit is unpalatable," told Harlot thoughtfully, after the newcomer had licked her face and she had licked her lips in reaction.

Nevertheless, with much affection, they all stroked the animal's main, while untangling the many Elf Locks that had been placed about.

"If only I knew how to mount a mare, how wonderful it would be," assured the girl aloud, in a melancholic fashion.

The animal however did not mind that Harlot did not know how to ride her kind. Thus, with little effort, the girl placed herself upon the mare's back, followed by the others, and they all rode together.

A wonderful time they had, where many adventures were taken. They passed Kreggles and Greners, Moon-Tots and Krenners, some of which partook in breakfast at noon and dinner at dawn, and other things like that.

After much and many a journeys, Harlot spotted something particularly lovely in the distance.

"What is that I see in the distance? How lovely," announced the girl.

Not too far off was an abode that looked kind enough to welcome a stay.

And so, in that direction they went.

A few stones throw away from the house of hospitality, the beings happened to pass an ugly man dressed in a lavish array of conventional garments and delicately scented pocket-candles, which caused him to appear like a trustworthy gentleman and not of the ugly looking sort. Nevertheless, he was ugly, very ugly; he was hawking what he liked to call 'things.'

"Come see my things," announced the ugly-man. "I have so many different things. Things for everyone for every need."

"Those are not things," told the Faerie.

"Oh, but that is to the fool's lazy eye," responded the ugly-man. "Come and look closer. I will make you a bargain you will never refuse. Look here." The ugly-man walked onto a small platform and brought over one of his 'things' by its knotted hair and then continued. "You see, tell me you would not shout with joy by seeing such a thing."

The ugly-man brought each of the 'things' out one by one, while proclaiming they were of his finest stock. When finished, and all were placed into a line, Blue Spek took out the ugly-man's eyes with her fingers and threw them into the dirt. The ugly-man soon expired, and the beings were freed from this specific situation.

A glorious moment indeed!

As Harlot and her friends went on towards the house of hospitality, with the continued aid the mare, another event occurred, causing a momentary delay; it was the cause of a gathering of pixies. The beings had lovely faces and fingers and noses and necks and ears and eyes and toes and teeth and backs and bottoms and chests and cheeks and legs and lips and heads and hands and many more and more and more; but most importantly, the beating beneath their breasts were the most lovely.

All together, the pixies frolicked about the girl whispering, "Look! A pretty flower," they all agreed. "We must say our greetings and press lightly upon the darling beauty."

So all the pixies gave a pinch and the such, causing much a bruise. But Harlot felt pleased, for she was positively charmed by the delightful bodies before her, for the eyes of the lovelies were made of emeralds and feet of straw and toes of rocks, while all else was made of soft flesh and boxes of bone.

All gathered together, humming, singing, and drinking a liquid made within an Elf Cup, which everyone agreed to be positively delicious.

But alas, the event took so much time that when finished it was night.

After the telling of many stories, all went to sleep.

CHAPTER V

AT THE HOUSE OF HOSPITALITY

Once all awoke, and the pixies gave their saddening goodbyes, taking the mare with them, and thus no more pixie leadings came to be, the girl, the Faerie, the Nymph, and the Butter-Maiden arrived at the front of the house of hospitality.

It looked mightily grand, but humble.

"Come in," invited a wealthy-widow, standing by a door of the house; the woman was of old age, was dressed in bright coloured clothing, and was of high spirits: she had an unconventional independence. "I alone reside within this place, so you may feel free and comfortable to do and be as you please."

"It looks ever so nice from the outside. I do hope the inside is just as pleasing," exclaimed Harlot to no one in particular.

And it was.

That very day, a grand feast was set on the table for all, and delicious drinks were served as well. First, each of the beings washed their hands in a certain fashion and then sat down in whatever place they pleased, for they were all welcomed to wherever they wished.

After a lively preliminary conversation, the wealthy-widow asked for the gathering of the girl and the others, so

to join her in the carvings of the meats. There was game and
swine and foul, among others, all set up very life like, some
roasted, while others were cooked in all sorts of red sauces,
presented in all sorts of ways, including troughs.

All had plenty of each and everything that occupied the
never-ending deliciousness, which included, to name a few,
the likes of creamy rose tarts, one night mushroom pasties,
sweet and sticky and thick cherry pottages, ale-barm
cracknels, the whitest wastel ever seen, delightful paradise
herb fritters, and various assortments of the plainest of hard
and soft cheeses, as well as the thickest of caudles and a
claret as candied as gingerbread, all to be had whenever the
diners ever so happened to please, and to be enjoyed
through the use of whichever etiquette was thought suitable
at the moment, even the feeling fingers.

When it was time for a pause in eating, Blue Spek and
Pik-Pek put on a spectacle, which was then followed by the
continuation of the eating and drinking of the great feast,
and then the washing of hands once more.

"Little lady," whispered the woman to Harlot, when the
evening grew old, "I believe I will send myself to my own
chambers, but you are welcome to use this place however
you may please."

The girl became very much excited by this offer and thus
immediately went wandering about the house, but she soon
found nothing that fancied her present interests.

"What a boorish place," complained Harlot to her
friends.

Then, as an inevitable consequence of the feast, the girl
became very thirsty, for she had taken quite a fancy to the
meats and sweets, whereas much of the former had been

well salted, and the later well sugared. Luckily, Harlot was able to find a bottle of liquid that looked like it had the potential of quenching her thirst.

And it did.

And things began to become quite interesting after that, for the girl and for the others.

In-side and out-side, on-side and bellow-side, Harlot's eyes went slivering onto the walls and up upon the floor that now seemed much more noteworthy to look upon and within than before. At certain times, the girl made humming sounds and mazes with what she said, but most of the time she went about looking through things she had thought had not deserved a first glance when seen a second time for the first.

"I think—" began Harlot, before she was cut off by a troubling situation.

Wherever the girl went a shadow followed. Though she stomped on the intrusion a few times, in frequent successions, it continued to wallow towards her, up and over, through both rooms and the places she travelled. Harlot tried to breath the shadow in as hard as she could, but that did not work either. Blue Spek and Pik-Pek laughed at the sight, and so did Lady. For a reason, the girl tried laughing as well; the situation then seemed more bearable.

Spaces and places and things in general pleasantly came and passed by as the beings tried to make themselves from one location and situation to another.

There was a moment when Harlot thought she saw the Faerie find a fish and eat its insides with a drip of a type of flavour adding sauce.

Then there was another moment when the girl thought she saw the Nymph sitting on top of a window's ledge, chanting a very silly song, first pointing at herself, then towards the outer side of the window:

Pockets! Pockets! Pockets!
Swing a wing a locket
Lock it! Lock it! Lock it!
Ring a ring'n dock it

Tidily say can
Diddle! Diddle! Diddle!
Tidily say and
Swindle! Swindle! Swindle!

Then there was another other moment when Harlot thought she saw the Butter-Maiden picking at a pile of needles upon the ground near a little apple tree, one spitting its silver roots down, down, down.

In any event, as the girl continued on, many colours plastered themselves to her vision. She felt them all around her waist and face, dripping onto the floor and walls and way up to the trotting lights placed there and there.

"Hmm, what is that over there?" wondered Harlot aloud.

It was a goat sitting on a high-headed chair making custard, but not the type that taste like overcooked dirt because it has spent too much time over a flame. No, this goat looked quite tasty. The custard however appeared to be more desirable to the girl's tongue at the moment, and it was already prepared; so she took a great mouthful of the usually delicious desert.

Though Harlot was set to verbalized her reaction to what she had just put into her mouth, she was delayed by the interruption of the animal's gruel-brained protestations: its chair was much to high and its head could never reach the top. The goat whimpered and violently ground its lips at this, devoutly frustrated, and then, in a moment of inspiration, it flung its head over the highest part of the chair with such a fierceness that it did indeed accomplish its much desired task.

And so there was no more goat, only meat.

When the girl was finally able to speak, and no interruptions continued, she announced to the custard's still maker, "I have to say, custard is just wonderful, but this stuff tastes awful."

But as no response came, Harlot carried on with her wanderings, roaming a circle of a few feet, until becoming fixed with the wish of protecting her dress from the recently spilled red that puddled about. So she whirled herself round and round, laughing as barrels of colours spilt from her sides, splashing themselves onto the walls, mixing into and covering up all the redness.

For no particular reason, the girl stopped laughing and instead screamed as hard as she could, but no one heard, for she was doing so in her head. With a dry throat from the demanding exercise, she searched and then found and then drank another delicious liquid refreshment, then continued on with her twirling for many more moments, eventually meeting a handful of stars, ones that had made themselves through a few windowpanes and into the house's walls.

They all turned together, shining and shining and shining. Harlot made the most of the moment and let the bursts of lights shine on as much of her as they possibly could, all while she danced with flailing hands and hair.

Eventually, the girl made herself outside and was quickly joined by the others, who then all played in the star lit grass; how much softer and wetter grass is at night, they all thought together.

After swishing in the sparkling dew, Harlot, Blue Spek, Pik-Pek, and Lady went back into the house, found a bed, went into it as they were, for that was custom, and then fell sleep.

CHAPTER VI

A KNIGHT AND HIS SWORD

"What a delightful morning," announced the girl, as she awoke to the sights and sounds of singing birds, flowers spreading themselves open by the slightest touches of the cock-crow's sun, and the drippings of dew from that of Nature's makings, all occurring inside the room she had been sleeping in.

Once fully ready eyed and minded, there was more delicious food to be had from that of the wealthy-widow. Yet, regretfully, as eating commenced, their feast was ruddily interrupted by the sound of banging on a door: A knight, tall on his horse, stood on the other side, looking for a place to take him in with hospitality.

"Of course, come in," invited the wealthy-widow, for she had an exceedingly giving heart. "Take what food upon the table you desire. As you eat and drink, I will bring your horse some refreshments as well."

And thus, when the woman departed to do her promised duty, the man searched around the house. Not long into his peeping, he noticed Harlot and the others peeking out from behind the corner of a wall.

"Come here my fair maidens," told the knight.

So they did, for the wealthy-widow's reception gave the impression that knights are of the noble sort.

After all gave their curtsies or bows, the man fell onto both knees and lamented: "Oh fair and beautiful. I am dreadfully sick. Both my mind and body do not do well. It is as if I have been struck through the heart by a poisonous dagger, now lurking unseen in the darkness, readying for its final blow. I need your remedy, your cure. Only you have the power to save me from a vicious demise. Though it annoys me to say that I cannot take it from you, I plead to my dear maiden and tell her that I am your dutiful servant, one who hopes to attain your honesty as a reward. The pain! The pain! Oh how my heart pangs inside this prison. Be my physician and save me from sickness and distress."

The girl, the Faerie, the Nymph, and the Butter-Maiden looked at one another, and then asked the knight to whom he was speaking.

"To you of coarse," replied the man.

"And who is that?" one of them enquired.

The knight seemed dissatisfied at this answer, for he expected them all to be his deliverer, and so he recited his speech, word for word, once again.

During the time of silence that followed the repetition, the woman appeared and announced to the man, "Your room has been prepared."

"Thank you my dear widow," sounded the knight in a heroic voice. "My body needs a place to rest, for it feels so very weak. If only a virtuous maiden would be so kind as to save a burdened soul. She knows where I will be."

All quit any listening to the man for the rest of the day, as he was quite annoying, and highly dramatic, persistently reciting his supposed grievances; nevertheless, the house was filled with merriment and dancing while he was away.

When evening came, each partook in the grandest of feasts anyone could ever behold; yet, on this occasion, the knight took charge of the meal and placed himself at the head of the table, carving all the meats he entitled himself to first.

After the courtly-knight's stomach was full, he stood up and lamented, "Though this feast has filled my stomach, both my body and mind thirst for something else. The pain is too much for me to bare."

The courtly-knight brandished a portion of his sword from its sheath, then indignantly retreated to his room.

The next day, the house was again filled with merriment and dancing.

When evening came, each partook in the grandest of feasts anyone could ever behold.

After the courtly-knight's stomach was full, he stood up and lamented again, "Though this feast has filled my stomach, both my body and mind thirst for something else. The pain is too much for me to bare."

The courtly-knight brandished an even greater potion of his sword from its sheath, then indignantly retreated to his room.

The next day, the house was again filled with merriment and dancing.

When evening came, each partook in the grandest of feasts anyone could ever behold.

After the courtly-knight's stomach was full, he stood up and lamented for the final time, "For three nights, I have eaten a grand feast like no other, but another hunger has not been satisfied. I now declare that the pain in me I will no longer bare. It shall be finished before the cock's crow at dawn."

The courtly-knight brandished his sword in its entirety, erected it towards everyone other than himself, and then caused the occupants of the house to play a game of hide and seek; he was it. Harlot and the others became so enthusiastic by the thought of a game that each ran into a separate room, hoping to become sole champion.

The Butter-Maiden's tale: Lady ran into a room that was filled with many different sorts of furniture, such as drawers and cushions. Though the opportunities were vast, she decided to try and hide herself underneath a bed that was in the midst of leaking feathers. However, such a place was much too difficult to breath underneath; therefore, the Butter-Maiden shuffled the fallen feathers to her sides, and then a dark hole appeared. So she crept into it.

The Ground Faerie and the Wood and Water Nymph's tale: Blue Spek and Pik-Pek were going to find their own hiding places separately, but in the end they went looking together. When they made themselves into a kitchen, both became delighted at the finding of a pile of onions, one that would eloquently hide their bodies ever so nicely. However, as the Faerie and Nymph crackled their way in, they realized that the onion skins made the loudest of noises with even the smallest of movements, and they did not intend to stay still; therefore, as the two tried to find their way out, pressing one another up against a wall, a dark hole appeared. So they crept into it.

The girl's tale: Harlot led herself into a closet that seemed to cloister her inside: the ceiling was too low, the walls were too close to one another, the floor was too high, the shelves were too crowded, the lighting was not dark enough, and the air was making her feel a little faint, but she decided that the place would be sufficient for her cause. However, when the girl flailed her arms about in order to keep herself occupied, an assortment of fabrics fell, burying her underneath; therefore, as Harlot tried to find a way through and out of the debris, she took hold of a particular cloth, and a dark hole appeared. So she crept into it.

The man's tale: The courtly-knight searched and searched, desperately trying to find those he had wiled into playing his sport, but he soon turned into a rage, realizing that he was unable to find anyone. He shouted in frustration, but found no holes. However, as the courtly-knight hunted, eagerly brandishing his sword towards any hiding place that could be found with such an orientation, his self-serving intentions led him onto his own blade; therefore, unrealistically, it was his undoing. So he did not creep into it.

The woman's tale: During this time, the wealthy-widow placed her thoughts upon the game, aggravated by the latest newcomer, the one who had made himself ready to seize and steal any he desired to please his appetite with. She had thus made a soup especially for him. However, when the courtly-knight was unable to ingest it, the woman called out to the other guests of her house; but, when no answer came, she deduced they were no longer with her.

CHAPTER VII

TUNNELS AND TROLLS

It happened to be that each and every hole the girl and the others had made themselves into led to a joining pathway, which guided them to a dirt-covered room, which held a small inverted mound in the ground, which made them all sneeze uncontrollably for some time. Harlot decided to shout, and the others followed; it seemed to make the sneezing stop (as shouting often does). Since there was another tunnel at the opposite side of the room, they all made themselves into it, shouting all the while.

A shaded woodland eventually showed itself, and all around an uncanny theme played, like pockets of nutmeg buried deep in a pie. The bark and leaves of the trees where black, except for a few dark greenish blotches here and there; there were only a few seepings and sweepings of light, which came from mischievous looking berries; and all this was accompanied by a thick layer of dust that busied itself like an edible pestilence, puppeting grey shadows, both in and not in the places shadows should be. Further within the woodland, lifeless bodies methodically swayed from twisted ropes, each jerking erected sticks with hopeful intentions towards any fair passerby that might pass close enough; the girl, the Faerie, the Nymph, and the Butter-maiden did not pass close enough.

The following occurred: The dark trees took hold of themselves and changed in shape and colour; they were no longer trees, but instead one large and spacious cave, lit by burning feathers that whistled as they fell from jagged candy-cane like structures upon the ceilings.

"Ra-chachachacha," was a noise that sounded, followed by many more similar sounds.

From the far west of the cave, a horde of small cloaked and crouching trolls were slowly making themselves into Harlot's direction; each and every one was aided by a walking cane in both of their hands, and a metal weaved sac laid upon their backs, which seemed to burn with a brightness from something inside. Though the creatures were only a few paces away from the other cave dwellers, the beings were not detected; in actuality, the trolls no longer had any eyes, only tar laid where those things use to be. They were withal blinded by their feverous desires.

And so, the creatures pressed themselves forth, without the possibility of interruption, towards a tall stone hut handsomely decorated in a delicate and warm raspberry like sauce.

One at a time, after entering and exiting the mentioned construction, each of the trolls brought out an armful of bones, partially covered in some sort of edible tissue; they tore off what they could eat, placed whatever it was into clay bowls, then fed, using one of the many spoons they carried upon themselves. It was quite evident that the creatures had recently come to their moving forms from those of stone, for their appetites were great and the moss and shrubs upon their skin were bountiful; one even had a nest of birds upon its head, which was quickly stuffed into a mouth when discovered.

The trolls ate their products of nourishment to the utmost extant, grumbling sounds as they did their biddings. Yet, once all within the hut was consumed, the creatures began to shriek and stomp their feet in a hysterical manner; they were still insatiably hungry.

In consequence, the following occurred in order to attain satisfaction: Each took out a burning torch from within the metal weaved sacs upon their backs; then, they cut off bite-sized pieces of whoever was in the closest proximity, gurgling in sounds of both pleasure and that of pain; then, they cooked the morsels of acquired flesh with the help of the flaming sticks; and lastly, munching ensued.

Because of the inexplicable influences of the scene, the beings also became hungry; but instead of eating one another, for none wanted to be eaten, they quit any such thoughts, looked for a moment, exerting a degree of effort, and found a grand table before them filled with fruits and delicacies of many different kinds.

Only then did they eat.

"I love the taste of bluternutberry," told Blue Spek.

"I love the taste of whatever this is," told the girl.

And they all ate and ate, making sounds of 'mmm' and 'mmm' until they were interrupted by the cries of the foul trolls.

"Ri-chachachacha," sounded one.

"Wa-jajajaja," noised another.

It happened to be that the crouching creatures had gotten carried away with their eating and had partook in every last bit of their neighbours as was possible. Each could hardly move; more precisely, each did not have anything to move, except for some parts of a mouth and some bones.

As this situation presented itself, another horde of small cloaked, crouching, cane holding trolls, who looked somewhat similar to the last, silently approached from the east side of the cave. Yet, on this occasion, the beings were noticed because of the sounds they had been making during their own eatings. The creatures advanced some more, then began to motion their intentions, for they seemed to be unable to speak.

Alas, after gesticulations, the trolls quaffed down a few buckets of grog to wash away any superficially irksome hesitations, and then Harlot and her companions were taken and pressed into a tight box, about three feet, by two feet, by some (that is by height, by width, and by length).

"This is just terrible," exclaimed the girl, with much anxiety and tears.

Indeed it was.

The creatures were vain things and boasted of their achievements as they pursued. First, the trolls paraded about, snarling and spitting all over the box; then, one by one, they took their precious canes and forced them into any crack they could, which inevitably ripped and went deep into the box, stabbing Harlot and the others with such a fierceness that it caused many a mark upon their tender bodies. After a short yet eternal while, the canes let out a substance that filled the box up and up towards the very top. It was a vile matter, like that of rancid milk sludge.

"Yuck! Yuck! Yuck!" they all gaged and sounded.

To the beings' dismay, though some of the liquid dripped its way outside of the box, most stayed within, causing there to be only a small amount of air to breath from. The Faerie tried blowing out what was within her lungs in order to push away the liquid that was choking her, but even after the friends joined in, blowing with much determination, exhaustion and dizziness ensued, and so the air seeped away while the liquid continued to dominate their space.

"What shall we do now?" questioned Harlot aloud.

Blue Spek suggested another idea: "We must gulp the liquid down and fill ourselves up instead of the box."

Thus, they all did as the Faerie proposed and tried to swallow as much of the sludge as possible; but there was just too much.

"There is just too much," shouted the girl, with her mouth full and leaking, while her stomach swelled, turning out with a round bump.

After seeming defeat, the feeling of devastation and guilt took over.

Yet, Harlot, in a last action of despair, managed to grab one of the creature's cane, which had continued to make its way into the box, and, to her surprise, and everyone's around her, she broke the thing in half. The others, with invigorated expressions, joined in the task of eliminating the remaining canes that also continued to force themselves into the box (for elimination is the only way to get rid of such things, and it brings some justice). The beings broke one here, and then another when it went over there; in the end, they broke every cane that made its way towards them, which was all. Each troll let out surges of great cries, all the while complaining, for they could talk, that such treatment was unfair and unwarranted, and what they had done was not that serious, only a little bit of fun, and that what they had done was in their nature and so should be viewed as acceptable (which is an orthodox and accepted argument).

In any event, after obtaining a piece of redress, the girl devised an idea that she and the others should use their own hands and press against the insides of the box in order to enable them their innate freedom.

With proper maneuvering, the box burst open.

The creatures stood staring at the persons before them, then laughed; however, when the trolls opened their mouths, bits of the substances from their canes slipped inside; they all then choked and dropped onto the ground, lifeless. (One more piece of justice was achieved, though it can never be completely obtained.)

"Look at that," directed Harlot.

For at this time the feathers within the cave began to fall in greater numbers, landing onto the bodies of all the still creatures, which caused them to burst into flames and give off an awful stench. After awhile, when there was nothing left of those despicable things, except the dust of their bones, starting with the girl, they all jumped and played in the dustiness that littered the ground.

(As the reader has most likely learnt thus far, honest situations do not last. And this time was of no exception.)

CHAPTER VIII

A HORDE OF ALTER FOPS WITH CROWS ON THEIR HEADS

After a not so long moment, something happened, something indeed. One, two, three, all the way to twenty, there came prancing into the cave, with haughtiness for eyes and vanity for smiles, black tainted pietists draped in glorious garments of white. Each one of them, the so called Crowned-Alter-Fops that is, had three jeweled crows upon their heads, one on top of the next, with a gold key in one hand and a silver in the other, which were used to enter wherever and whatever they wished; the men carried nothing else, particularly a hidden tree. Their vestments were exceedingly lavish, like a barrel full of the richest icing, the type specially used for rotten cake. Each dragged a collection of texts by a long rope behind themselves, which the creatures used, but only certain pages and parts, for the projecting of their voices and personal agendas.

"You, common cattle," commenced the one with the biggest crows and the longest clothes and the biggest jewels. "What are you doing?"

Harlot looked at the man with justified eyes of inquiry; however, before she could respond, another servant of servants, one that had a smaller crow and shorter clothes and smaller jewels, spoke in a condescending manner, "You may respond without your head."

"I will speak with my head thank you very much. You cannot have it, nor will I give it too you willingly. And for our situation, we were bouncing on the dust of the terrible trolls before you all came about," told and explained the girl, as she proudly stomped around some more.

The fumbling-keepers readjusted the crows upon their heads and then gathered themselves into a circle. They waved through the air funny smelling smoking sticks, read some parts from the books they handled wherever they went, ate a few goblet-grape pies with their fingers, then walked around humming in low pitches.

"Come here girl," demanded the Alter-Fop who had spoken first. "I will give you something."

"Presents! I love presents! I do believe I should receive present more often, whether during the day, evening, night, or at any time for that matter. In fact, I do not receive enough. Now give me my presents!" exclaimed, assured, and then commanded Harlot.

At this, the man took from his pocket a green hood and a long white piece of wood. He presented it before the girl with the following words: "Take it."

Harlot looked at the large Crowned-Alter-Fop and what he had put before her; she was much displeased.

"This is no present! This is just terrible. Just terrible. Do you have anything better? I would much rather something else," affirmed the girl.

"No, I do not," scolded the large three-crowed man. "And this is no present girl. Take it now."

But Harlot did not.

"You must excuse the awkwardness of the situation," craftily interjected a much more tolerable looking Crowned-

Alter-Fop, one who seemed much more trustworthy than the others; he had pockets full of butterscotch balls. "Have some of these delicious sweets of mine. They will please you to the uttermost extant."

Of coarse such butterscotch balls were of the best of kind. Just one of those magnificent little jewels could make one's entire mouth water down to their toes, and two of them to one's nose.

The beings joyously chewed the flavourful candies until their jaws became sore and could move no longer.

"Tell me girl," began the man who had given the candies, "where do the doves go when they are done their fluttering?"

Harlot tried to respond, but she could not; her mouth was much too tired and had not enough animation left in it to produce even a few words.

"Ha!" exclaimed the Alter-Fop with the largest crows. "I told you so."

"I knew it was so from the very beginning," assured the smartly sly one. "She has no head. She is but a common slag."

The girl, made anxious by the repeated remarks of her having no head, began to run about looking to see if she could find a reflection, one that could tell her if it was really there or not. At last, by the hut of the trolls, she found a red pool; it reassured her.

However, Harlot could not correct the Crowned-Alter-Fops for their heedless observation, for her whole company and herself were suddenly bound and put into one of the metal sacks of an expired troll, which was not comfortable in the least. The girl made her discomfort known, but her distress did not change the course and matters of the minds of the horrible things.

"What an uncomfortable place to be," voiced a being.

"Terrible," told another.

Yet, within Harlot's plackets was a pleasant place to be, so the Faerie and Nymph positioned themselves within. The Butter-Maiden was also uncomfortable, but she was much too big to fit herself into any placket Harlot had upon herself; the girl was met with the same difficulty.

So the two laid upon one another as much away from the terrible sack as they could, and soon began to dream a dreadful dream, but a living one nonetheless.

The Dream of the Sack

There was a market filled with fruit, without any sound, quite, mute.

Long had this place been forgotten, the birds had left, harvests rotten.

Two women they fiddled, without any strings, inside a home, inside their rings.

So blissful they did play, to sounds of ancients, each and each both, filled with patients.

When the time came, the women they cried, then opened their mouths, shout out and died.

Out from a place, came wonders of green, out came the birds, and out came a stream.

Like milk upon a castle rock, a glorious sight, filled their smocks.

But alas, this ended, for there came a man of art, singing a song, and pulling a cart.

"Come here," he demanded. "I shall seize you both at once, claim my farthing, for I am no dunce."

The women they shivered, quietly they swooned, no more freedom, misogyny tuned.

So to the cart they went, and swiftly abased, scalded in turns, for they were disgraced.

CHAPTER IX

OUT OF THE SACK

The dreadful ending of the dream lasted for quite a long while, brought only to a close by the dropping and opening of the sack, and the plucking out of its 'contents.'

One by one, the beings found themselves on a path of dirt.

To the left stood a precipice, decorated beyond with purple mountains made of women's bane and forget-me-nots, bumping on and about like dozens of fresh falling eggs, laid by the most delicate of infinite singing birds. While to the right was a laborious and extravagant palace-cave made of crystal and the reddest of meats, one coupled with forever flowing honey fountains, molasses vines, sugar twigs, and a line of large luxurious looking beds: the laters having thick feathered beddings supported by a pair of fresh woolen mattresses, a collection of feathered bolsters lined with the most exotic of furs and covered with the softest of silken head sheets, and similar coverlets and feather filled blankets as well. All this was shaded by a surrounding collection of many trees and perfumed by what could only be described as honeyed gold.

The men of the cave spent much of their time piously observing veiled figures rowing upon a nearby river, one flowing with that of milk, wine, and honey, and the shedding of any harborous deceivers of cloaked desire. How the watchers enjoyed the tempting rays made by the exposing sun, and the revealing flapping breathed by the breezing winds, waiting to catch a sight and grasp one of those heathens, hoping to teach them how to properly pray.

It was a world where no man worried about the difficulties of life: dirt, disease, or demure. A place night never touched, every desire fulfilled, no rain made a moment dreary, nor any flea upon even the very tip of an eye lash could be found.

It was a place of complete pleasure, for all the senses.

"I thought it would be night, or at least evening for that matter, but there is daylight. It must be noon," thought Harlot aloud, trying to push away the thought of the dream and the sack.

Indeed it was noon, for the sounding of ringing bells said it was so, and whatever they say is said to be indisputable.

And, with each toll, liquorish Monks came parading out from the palace-cave, one covered with a tree filled with all the most exotic of spices from every known and unknown place, in order to meet with the Crowned-Alter-Fops. The fat men were exceedingly gluttonous creatures: though each wore a dark, thick, and large one pieced robe, one could see their stomachs protruding out from underneath. They had no beards on their cheeks; the hair on their heads were finely combed within fashionable tonsures; and they had clean looking feet, though their faces and hands were filthy with stickiness from the honey and sweet things they constantly consumed.

The girl and the others were taken and bound to a nearby bed with ropes previously used to entertain at the gallows. The monks were quite excited by the arrival, as they believed the beings must have strayed too far from their abbey during one of their carnal boat rides upon the rivers of sweet milk, and now there was no need to take flight and swoop down themselves, for everything they wanted was now before them.

The free-ones then began preparations for the month of honey, chanting 'In His name,' over and over again, as if they said it enough times it was thus true. All the men hierarchically said what they said should be said, things they said should be said when they said should be said and said and done, and then the fat men brought out great barrels of mead. As time went one, more and more barrels were brought, and then more barrels were needed, for as soon as a barrel came out it was immediately emptied and a full one was expected in its place. There were honey delicacies of every kind, starting with biscuits and cakes and soups and stews, to everything anyone could ever produce, all made from the flowing honey fountain that never ran dry. There were even roasted garlic geese and cinnamon and clove larks that flew through the air, landing straight into the mouths of the men. How they very much did enjoy this.

Eventually, when all the barrels within close proximity were emptied, which was a disruption to every caroler present, the creatures with the crows and the fat things from the cave sang this honest song:

Out from paradise we take our mutton,
Away from the little ones, even their buttons.
So cold and still they lay in their beds,
But we sing and dance and laugh in our heads.

(An interlude of laughing in song form.)

Then when you're quite
And our pockets are filled,
Your words are nothing
And worthless still.
But do not forget
To pay your rent.
Another cup!
A day well spent.

After their frankness, the men looked at Harlot, Blue Spek, Pik-Pek, and Lady, all bound to the beds, and then each gave a long and inglorious speech.

When this had finally come to an end, one Monk dropped to the floor, then another, then a Crowned-Alter-Fop, and then more and more, until all the men laid on the ground without any breath; they had had too many barrels.

A gluttonous cause for the ending of them all.

"How are we to get ourselves off and away?" questioned the girl, much annoyed that she could not move most of the parts of her body.

No one produced an idea to share, so they laid in silence for some while.

CHAPTER X

AND THEN ANOTHER OTHER

"Is it time for biscuits and butter already?" queried something or someone at a certain time.

"Butter and biscuits would be ever so nice, but I do believe there is nothing of the sort left," answered Harlot, though she did not know who or what she was talking to.

"I believe you are mistaken," responded the thing or someone. "There is indeed a meal. But where to start the relish? Over here where the grass grows like liquorish weeds on a windowsill? But I hate liquorish. Ghastly, ghastly stuff indeed. Oh! Or perhaps over there, where none grows at all? That seems better, like slipping into butter. Yes, much better indeed. But wait, should I go where it is straight and smooth? Or where the silk flutters out in cream filled ripples and wishes to be played like a wanting fiddle? I can just imagine one to the other, or one and the other. Oh my! Oh my! Such a selection, not enough time."

Jumping sounds were heard; the speaker then continued.

"This is all getting to me. I must sit down. I must take a breath. And breathe and stop. And breathe and stop…Aha! I have come to a conclusion. This is excellent indeed. I always surprise myself when I put my thinking to it.

"Alright, Alright," assured the creature or thing to itself. "I must hurry. But wait. Is this the place? Oh dear! I believe

I have misplaced myself of where to go. But halt I say. I cannot give up. No. I must keep my faith and go forth to the task. Yes! Haha! Indeed."

At this point, whatever or whoever the voice was coming from began to play many a fine instruments. Perhaps a trumpet played, or perhaps some sort of other wind musical instrument piece, but definitely not a flute.

Then it or they went on self-conversing in a higher manner of intellect of words: "This prompts me to recollect a time, oh how it was ever such a time, when I happened, which I may call fated-chance, to stumble onto something very similar to this situation. It was nearly dusk outside, and I had lost something but could not figure out what it was that I had misplaced; so I searched about for much a long time. I eventually encountered a strange creature that was sitting by a stone covered in some sort of paint of some colour. It asked me in a whisper, 'Would you care for something hot or something cold?' At first I presented myself as if I had the slightest idea of what it was insinuating. 'Do you mean to offer a heated cup of tea or something chilled like iced-chocolate?' I replied. But of coarse I could not keep up the deluding for very long without a slight effort, for I was indeed aware where I had brought myself, intentionally I must admit.

"So I told whatever it was, 'I have yet decided.' This prompted it to ask me: 'Would you care for something fresh or something told?' But again I spoke with words that reflected a mind of uncertainty. 'Then come and take a look and see,' it invited me, with its hands waving towards the place it had come from. And so I followed it.

"After shadowing for a time, I was, as I am now, taken aback with what beheld my eyes. First I looked about and saw one that reminded me of milk, and how soothingly it could cover the bodily soul. But then I approached in another direction and was met with an alternative that was wild and untamed, yet smoother than any other; nevertheless, I went on, wondering if the sights would continue on as they were.

"'Would you care for something of the outside or that of the in?' it asked in a restless whisper, losing some composure. My nerves, how they rapa-tat-tated within me throughout; I was certainly in a precarious position. All mattered on what there was and what I wished to know. Yet, I was met face-to-face with an indecision, such was the brutality of my situation, one all men face in such a scene. Oh how I wished to roam the countless edges that had never been seen, blowing onto its unknown peeks and passes, knowing that unchanged scene; yet, I was taken aback by another sight that caught my eyes more than any other."

"'Come on now,' interrupted the purveyor. 'You must make a match. Time is slipping, so get on with your visiting.' Oh how the ghastly fool caught me off guard. How despicable. What nerve, I thought. But alas! There before me—"

Blue Spek, aggravated by what she was hearing, shouted out, "Untie us this very instant you ferocious façade."

"Indeed," was the response.

No one gave an answer.

"Indeed," was the response.

No one gave a word.

After this went on some more, something happened, though no one knew what exactly.

The girl began to feel a puddle of liquid forming itself around her feet. When she tried to get herself away from the wetness, she discovered something had broken the rope that had bound her feet, as well as whatever or whoever had been speaking.

"This is quite a happenstance for you my dear feet and legs, but there is still much of me confined," told Harlot to her partially unfettered self, while giggling at the thought of receiving a reply from her own parts.

Though the girl was a little more unrestrained than the others, she was still unable to move with complete freedom: her shoulders and wrists were still tightly confined to the bed.

"Come on toes, you can do it," assured Harlot to herself, as she reached with her feet fingers above her head, pouncing her knees against her chest, trying to fold herself in half, in hopes of untying those awful ropes. Inevitably, the girl's dress fell onto her face, causing her to scream out with much anxiety, for some of the wetness had made itself onto her clothes and had wet her face in result. Harlot blew and blew as hard as she could until the fabric became dry; this made her much more relaxed.

Commencing again, the girl wiggled herself back and forth, much like two lollipops playing in the wind, continuing on with her attempt to free her bounded parts. The situation proved to be much more difficult than Harlot had anticipated before beginning, but she persisted with great determination, legs stretched, extended towards her freedom.

Alas! The girl unbound herself, then the others.

CHAPTER XI

THE MILK MAIDENS

After Harlot, Blue Spek, Pik-Pek, and Lady had spent a commonplace journey along a path, which mostly consisted of the walking sort of events, a particular night fell upon them: The Butter-Maiden spotted, through the mouth of a pale tabernacle, three snowy white Milk-Maidens, all of whom were drawing milk. The beautiful beings had skin as snowy and smooth as well whipped egg whites, and the hairs upon their heads were as pleasing to the eyes as edible ivory. Each wore a white silken gown that covered their delicate shoulders, arms, and backs, thus not to hinder their milking, which they enjoyed, and so did as often as they desired; their limbs were slender and their eyes were made of red roses; and each was gathered around a single copper candle that pushed away the surrounding darkness of the night.

"My, look at them," gasped the girl, when they had all made themselves inside of the tent and in front of the Milk-Maidens; the indefinable sight captured Harlot.

Indeed a pleasure to behold.

"They are making cheese," educated the Faerie, caring for the girl's questioning temperament.

"How delightful, I want to make cheese too. It looks ever so delightful," voiced Harlot.

"You cannot," responded Blue Spek. "But you can watch."

"What! Why can I not make cheese? I can; I know I can," exclaimed, probed, and then assured the girl, feeling quite anxious.

Though Harlot had become passionately concerned with the thought of making cheese, briefly attempting it herself, at the moment she much preferred placing her eyes upon the enchanting beautiful beings. She watched as the Milk-Maidens procured and besprinkled the appetitive substance with delicately placed fingers, filling many buckets.

After much of the creamy nectar was drawn, all was placed, drip by drip, onto a bundle of suspended and heated rocks. First, an invigorating mist of scent made its way throughout, and then, slowly, the substance fell into a stone bowl below, each individual drip collecting itself in the form of a roundish ball.

Once all the milk had made the journey, the beautiful beings graciously fingered the little egg like creations, much more gracefully than kneading, for that maneuvering can be quite barbaric at times, and a wondrous cheese came to be.

"I want to make cheese! It looks ever so delicious," declared the girl, again, excited and invigorated by all the present occurrences.

"You cannot," rudely educated the Faerie, again, significantly upset that her watching had been interrupted.

But Harlot did not listen to such words again, and so she tried and tried, again and again, pressing herself beyond comfortable measures in order to reach her goal; but in the end, she could not make cheese as the Milk-Maidens did.

Though she did not understand why, even if she believed she could, faith and determination were useless.

In a hysteria of grief, the girl placed herself with arms and legs spread wide open upon the ground, much like a gingerbread biscuit, shed tears of innocence, and then contorted herself with an impressive dexterity.

When the beautiful beings witnessed the event, concern naturally followed; each agreed to give Harlot a nibble of the product they had made, instead of ignoring the reality around them.

"My goodness, this is delectable," declared the girl, as she gobbled down the sweet nourishing substance.

And naturally, the Milk-Maidens were pleased that Harlot was no longer distressed, so they allowed her some fresh warm milk too.

"My goodness gracious me, this tastes wonderful. It is so sweet. I am really enjoying myself. I really am," avowed the girl, as she lapped as much milk as she desired, trying not to let any of the white creaminess drip down her cheeks from her lips; though, when they did, she caught them all with an appointed finger and then placed them back into her mouth where they belonged.

To the interest and delight of the beautiful beings, Harlot had quite an insatiable appetite. Though the Milk-Maidens drenched her with enough substance to last a few blue moons, the girl desired more and more. To appease, a stone tub wide enough for several dozen gallons of liquid was brought forth and was then filled with mouthfuls of the beautiful beings' creamy substance, which covered Harlot's self completely and over ever so nicely. She then played, brushing her appetite, palming the warm milk to her cheeks and lips, moving her hands all about in round circular motions, swashing and jabbering, then Gulp! Gulp! Gulp! completely embracing herself within the whiteness she enjoyed ever so much. Harlot was quickly joined and an exciting milk-bout was had, followed by slumber.

When the girl awoke the next morning, daylight had begun peeking itself into the harbouring tent and into the eyes of its inhabitants. Before not too long, the beings rose, and the Milk-Maidens began the process of their making of cheese once again.

Oh how marvelous it was for all participants to partake in the wondrous feasts that continued to follow: milk and cheese and milk and cheese, for any moment of the day, for bathing and for eating, for pleasing and for pleasing.

But a time came when Blue Spek felt plajacent (You see, while it may continue to be a mysterious happening for many throughout, Faeries are known to partake in Faerie Rings, and when they do not do so on a regular basis, there is a tendency for agitation to develop. Now, since such a happening had not taken place for some time, Blue Spek's following words are quite understandable and undeniably expected): "I believe it is time for a Faerie Ring to be had."

As the Faerie looked quite troubled and determined to have her way, after enjoying some more of the delicious milk and cheese of the beautiful beings, followed by a teary eyed and lip goodbye, for the Milk-Maidens were not of the Faerie Ring partaking sort, the four made their way to the same path that had led them to such a delightful and rare encounter, and then walked and walked in another way.

When the time came that Blue Spek found an agreeable area between a collection of trees, she seated herself on the ground.

"Now what?" spit out Harlot, annoyed, for she wished to have stayed longer with the beautiful beings.

"We must wait until the stars become brighter and the spaces among the trees become tighter," told the Faerie, with much excitement.

There they all sat and waited, waiting for night to come.

End of Volume II

Volume III

CHAPTER I

THE FAERIE RING

And they waited and they waited.

"This is just ridicules," declared Harlot, for both the sitting still and anticipation made her fidgety and restless.

But on and on the waiting and waiting and waiting went.

Then evening came.

And, just as the last star appeared its brightest in the sky, the girl felt something underneath her, peaking itself out from the ground.

"No! I will not move. This is my place I tell you," cried out Harlot, with a firm resolution that whatever was moving beneath her would never cause her displacement, for she had declared that dwelling for herself first, and also, she had been sitting there for such a long time; so, she deserved that place.

Yet, whenever whatever it was continued on with its protruding, the girl wiggled her bottom back and forth, hoping the encroacher would place itself unto another area. When the situation proved stagnate, she increased her exertions and shook herself in all directions as wildly as she possibly could, jiggling and juddering about. When similar results resulted, Harlot raised herself off the ground, and then fell back onto her bottom with a tremendous force. That ploy did not aid in any way either; it simply hurt.

Suddenly, as the girl sat in silence, thinking of something else to try, scratching her thinking head and rubbing her sore self, a mushroom slipped itself out from underneath the ground and appeared between her legs.

"What an uncivil mushroom you are. Have you never heard of the common decency of sitting places? If I sit in a place first, then I get to sit there for as long as I like without any pushing away," professed Harlot, both pleased that she had won, but frustrated at what stood erect before her.

Nevertheless, the mushroom continued to give the impression that it had no intensions of moving away. So the girl placed both of her hands and all of her fingers around the intruder's stem and tugged at it with great determination; but, the mushroom did not release itself. When the first strategy showed an undesired result, Harlot tried to pick the thing apart with her fingers. When the second approach proved just as ineffective as the first, the girl attempted to tear the invader apart by thoroughly entrapping it with her teeth, followed with biting and biting, sinking it and her mouth bones down deeper and deeper. Harlot had to eventually put her hard working mouth to rest, for the mushroom would not move from its place, even if a little eaten.

Then she tried kicking it with her feet.

"Stop it!" demanded Blue Spek. "Look."

Many more mushrooms, much like the first, with its elaborate descriptiveness, were making their way out from underneath the ground, which was followed by the placing of themselves into the shape of a ring around the girl, the Faerie, the Nymph, and the Butter-Maiden.

And so the merrymaking began: Chanting and chanting and singing and dancing and shouting with sounds that echoed from there to there, and swaying and bouncing and playing in ways that made all within the Faerie Ring warm and delighted. There were mushrooms all around, some wiggling their heads, while others skipped or hopped about, around, and over. The dancing went on and continued, and minds soon joined in with the fluttering bodies.

In an appealing fashion, Blue Spek took off her crown and blew on it. Oh how it was of the grandest of moments, one that was to be told for time and time to come. The little Changelings, yes, each and every one of them, all across the land and all, were to try and tell and retell the story in all its majesty: On that particular night, when all else was wet, and more wetness was ready to come still, the Ground Faerie let forth her long streams of fluid. And how they twirled into and through the air, soon turning into deep and salient mists, like the round and round makings of Faerie floss.

Harlot, wrapped in the wetness, felt wonderfully pleased; so she breathed in as much as her lungs would let her, filling her chest with the marvelous spume. And around and down and down she felt, until she found herself passing through running water, and then an archway in the middle of a mound.

It was delightful.

On the other side of the place, the girl stumbled into a boat that had been battling a fearsome storm for much longer than is duly expected, overcoming waves the size of the likes of elephants on spits and spits in elephants, and bravely continuing on into the great unknowns, even at the threat of going up and up and then down and down into the depths below.

On the decks, as if on a hot fiery pan drenched with oil, fluctuated shaded figures, each with distinctive features and traits, such as this and that; the things were in the process of leaping into the feasting waters, calling out mumbling chants until they were no longer heard by even themselves.

In angst, Harlot took hold of several paddles that she had found tickling around her and threw them at the frightfully large waves, all the while calling out riddles and rhymes, sometimes two at a time.

The girl journeyed on, braving the untamed waters and the trunks of debris that floated by, ones that aimed at her all along the way, until she met a giant on a rock who told her to keep on with her dancing if she wished to keep her feet; so Harlot moved herself back and forth to the gestures and sounds she heard in her head, for she was much moved by the thoughts of losing her beautiful parts.

Spalsh! came a great wave, then Splush! came another; the storm continued on.

After long, and much dancing, the girl came to be inside of the ground, spending dedicated periods of time rubbing handfuls of dirt upon the walls of a delicately mossed cavern, one that stripped itself bare and unfolded at the lightest of touches.

The mentioned particular joyous situation did not last forever however, for Pik-Pek, at sometime, took Harlot by the hands and placed herself and the other on the top of an anxious seed, one which when dosed with a little water and sunlight grew into a fair sized tree, lifting the two higher and higher, as if such growing was all about its business.

When the occasion came that the tree was to be cut down, the girl and the Wood and Water Nymph made an away type of leap, landing into a warm pool of water as clear as combed nectar. There was much playing and swimming under and above one another, giggling and making teasing bubbles all the while. Yet, this came to an end when the water began to thicken with little shrubs, vines, and thorns, ones that slyly persisted in pushing towards the two swimmers. Taking a liking to Harlot, the plants crawled up her legs, grasping them firmly, and eventually decided to cover her body entirely. The girl thought she looked quite silly, Pik-Pek thought the same, especially when Harlot tried to move her legs back and forth with walking intentions, but could not.

Such situations continued on as the girl went from the hands of the Faerie to that of the Nymph's.

And then she once again joined the many mushrooms that continued to dance and sway within and upon the sides of the Faerie Ring. Harlot found it all quite stimulating, so she bounced about on her bottom, from one mushroom head to the next, while laughing and making other pleasing noises, swaying her limbs and singing and singing and singing.

One day, Harlot found a pile of stones with a wooden door in the middle. Wanting to enter, she made sure her hands were inviting, so breathed and breathed, filling all that was about with a warm steam. When ready, she caressed the outer frame, then took special care of the knob, like a tongue playing with a chocolate button, attentive not to bite down. The girl did this as she stroked and pulled with her other fingers about the door, ever so carefully, ever so gently.

And so it opened.

On the other side was an island containing many empty holes upon it, which would usually be judged as worthless until profited from; they were to be filled with things like dirt, corn cobs, fists full of carrots, lollypops, or candy-dots: an employment needed to be done according to doctrine. Yet, Harlot thought the holes pretty and perfect just as they were; they did not need anything else to be perfect.

And then something happened: Music. A drip, a drip of dripping water began to beat onto a drum, Tum! Tum! Tum! while the flowing locks of floating maidens played to the sounds of strumming harps. And Hums! and Hums! of choirs of doves fluttered in echoes and bounced into waving hands, turning into bright red leaves and yellow flowers, which then fell slowly and silently.

Unable to wait any longer, Lady took the girl by the hands and squeezed each of her fingers one by one, finger by finger, and then all together at once; Harlot could feel the buttery being squish through her palms, as if making piecrust with much more butter than was used as usual, making things much richer and much more fulfilling. And, as the Butter-Maiden buttered herself about, the white lead circles upon her fingers wandered around the girl: first they tangled themselves about her hair, but they quickly found themselves slipping to her lips, and then to one of her eyes; there was a desire for tree sap and its warm colour. (While a pocking in the eye may cause many to blink, Harlot enjoyed herself far too much to allow any distractions, though several tears did fall.)

Like bushels of herbs brought by the barrel full, a woodland of trees came wandering in on all sides, walking steadily, but not too hectically, from far and distant places, bunching themselves onto one another, all wanting to see the wonders of the Faerie Ring.

Harlot placed herself upwards, standing straight on her feet, then began to spin while calling out to those around her. Without much delay, she was joined by the hands of many wanting trees who swayed with the wind and the warmth of the stars above her.

While the girl enjoyed herself to the uttermost extent, when she grabbed Lady's silken gown, a great tear appeared. In a state, Harlot stopped her turning and stood still, staring at the Butter-Maiden; yet, such an incident did no cause a hindrance for the others that played, only the very opposite, for Lady received strength from the girl's doing, and so tore away the fabrics that bound and hid her, then continued on with the merrymaking.

And with more and more turnings and turnings, more and more became wondrous.

It was at this time that savoury droplets fell to the ground, splashing through all those around. The rounded waters quickly bubbled and stirred into the shapes of youngling flowers of all different kinds and colours. Each bud that made itself known seemed to use a spoon and whisper a little tale about how in a land where there was nothing but fresh and unadulterated substances, certain times could be spent frolicking without any worries that something may be prying from beyond a place not far from one's place.

Yet, while the realities of such thoughts were nonexistent, on and on the colours played, and the Faerie Ring went on and on, and on and on and on, and on and on and on, until it ended.

Harlot, Blue Spek, Pik-Pek and Lady then fell fast asleep.

CHAPTER II

THE WALLED GARDEN

When they had all risen from their slumber, the girl led herself into a fit of giggling. This went on for some time. The others watched, confused, wondering what deserved so much amusement.

"I had the silliest of dreams. I was on the top of a very large rock, drinking from a warm cup of broxy broth; but then all of a sudden, my bottom became slippery, and so I fell onto a pile of wax, and it was all sticky, just like molasses," told Harlot, laughing as she recounted and remembered the happening.

"Your dream sounds dull," responded the Faerie. "The one I had was much better."

The girl did not like Blue Spek's response in the least, so she continued to tell a part of her dream that she did not remember, speaking much louder than before.

"That is because you have not heard the whole dream. When I fell onto the pile of wax, a hat grew out from the ground and placed itself upon my head. Ha! A hat of all things. It could have been anything, but it was a hat, and a soft one at that," reassured Harlot, hoping the others would find what had supposedly happened to be as amusing as she thought it could be.

However, none seemed to share the girl's dream humour. So Harlot searched and searched with much effort, trying to find something that would catch the interest of her indifferent listeners.

She rummaged many possibilities for some time, even pioneering them all through a path and many other distances, which led through a trail of both squished and squirming bugs, then to another sight, one filled with broken snake cocoons and falling peach pits, which naturally led to another: a walled garden.

The girl was utterly pleased when the eyes of the Ground Faerie, the Wood and Water Nymph, and the Butter-Maiden gawked in delight at what they saw; but, to ill content, the garden was closed, and there seemed to be no way of entering inside of it.

"This is just terrible, just terrible," panicked Harlot.

But then, as they continued to circle the wall, getting to know the loveliness better, and becoming fine and well-intentioned acquaintances, the beings found a promising slit underneath a well-groomed bush, one that whispered to them in a fine tune to commence, and eventually come inside.

Seemingly narrow and tight at first, the tunnel soon stretched open and allowed the visitors to slip in with a wonderful ease. The girl was last to insert herself, for the excitement of them all had pushed her unto the behind.

Lady smiled, for there was much warmness and comfort inside. Blue Spek and Pik-Pek nodded to show that they agreed with the Butter-Maiden's observation. Yet, Harlot paid no attention to their agreeing with one another; she was much too excited by the fact that it was she who had found the place of interest, and thus the wonderful situation.

And deeper and deeper they all went, dancing in an amusing to and fro fashion, all the way along. At times, the pathway turned one way and then it turned to another, while at others it led the beings up and then down. Often, they found themselves moving around in circles, around and around and around, as if there was a serious task of the whisking of egg whites at hand, ones soon to be thick with firm puffing peaks.

Now and then, as it was a lengthy time, there was pausing, as rest is indeed an important occasion.

The pilgrims gleefully pressed on and through the dark and damp warmness, pushing further and further and further.

After a dexterous effort, they went up and up and onto the edge of a mound; each could feel that the garden was not much further away.

"How delightful that I found this place," voiced the girl, back to the others, after she had made herself the pioneer.

No one answered; they were all much too excited and in the midst of enjoying themselves: a promising slope stood before them.

And so slipping and sliding and climbing and dining, while screaming and shouting in utter delight, all went down and deeper into the tunnel, out towards the garden.

Then, in all of the moment's amazingness, while all were squeezing themselves together, contorting forward, this way and that, with such determination, marshmallow like crumbs spate upon them from behind, drooling and covering everywhere inside the tunnel entirely.

"This is delicious," announced Harlot, after her mouth had become full of the falling sticky sweetnesses.

And how wonderful it all was.

Indeed.

Then, immediately after, to each's relief, the devoted travelers spilled out of the tunnel and into the garden, immediately and completely basking in its marvelousness, like the likes of erecting fiddlehead ferns, baying upon lagoons full of wanting daisies, each dispersing blossoming pedals, one after another, counting whether it was to be true or not; and flappings of coconut palms, dropping and dividing their inner fruits to be drunken and nibbled on like a mid morning sweet brew; and the likes of a blade of lemon grass, one standing ever so heightened beyond the other limps surrounding it, soon to become one of them.

But alas, though the event and other sights were also of description, a tree in a corner of the garden held the girl's attention most firmly. It appeared to rise far above her head, up and up and up, and its roots far below her feet; yet, she could see every bit of it all at once, just as she could see the tips of her toes and the edges of her fingers when sitting in a tub full of fragrant and delicious rose water (though that had never happened).

At the very top of the tree were leaves that shimmered in the sunlight; they danced around the sky like little wisps of sugar flakes, ones soon to be melted onto something wet. Upon the roots that fell down and down and down into a never-ending pool of darkness, were pathways that never seemed to cease, similar to a bowl of plain black beans: they were trees without leaves, bending everywhere. In the middle was a trunk: it was brown and hairy, covered with little drops of liquid that were not at all pleasant to be around; it was not sap.

"I want to touch it," declared Harlot as she made herself towards the tree.

Yet, when she arrived, not too far from where the roots of the tree stood out, her feet, and then the rest of her, were forced to fall into the ground, even though she did not belong among them. The girl tried to grasp onto the roots as she fell, but they were much too thick for her hands to achieve any proper grip. Only after several trials and much effort, Harlot found a root and wrapped her arms and legs around it as tight as she could, though she continued to descend further and further into the ground.

Eventually, the girl had to stop, and so she did.

CHAPTER III

INSIDE THE GARDEN TREE

"Goodness," whispered Harlot to herself, not adding another word.

It was absolutely dark.

Though the girl was unable to see a single form about her, she bravely walked through the blackness, walking and walking, stopping, and then walking some more.

The ground made squelching noises. The air smelt like burnt biscuits. It tasted like them too. And after not a moment, the place began to become warmer and warmer.

Harlot made accommodations.

Soon enough, she tripped on something, and so fell into a shallow pit filled with a clammy substance, which conspicuously covered the front of her body almost entirely.

"This is just awful. Just awful," declared the girl, as she pressed herself out of the pool of stickiness.

But before she could even try to try to wipe the dreadful concoction off, she noticed something: a small flame between ripples and wrinkles of flowers laid in a near distance, and next to the sight was a bird with brightly coloured wings perched upright upon a stick.

The thing took flight and began to surround Harlot in repulsive consecutive circular motions, all the while spitting out pebbles and stones from its mouth (things that the consensus believed to be overly cracked and no longer of virtuous, or any moral, value).

The girl ran towards and gathered the fallen, then firmly held them against herself.

Many voices of laughter echoed in retort to her actions, each sound pairing itself with a handful of floating fingers, all pointing and jabbing wherever they pleased, pressing Harlot to the ground with a mighty force she alone could do nothing to overcome (as is strategically created systematically).

When the things grew bored, they left.

The girl raised herself up with a strength that is beyond comprehension, and continued on.

She took a step, and then another.

But before Harlot could take another other, an enticing well, one produced and procured from a specialty farm of its sort, was forcefully raised from underneath a hidden and sacred place. To her distress, Men-with-Sticks began to summit the walls of the well, pressing and planting their stiff bladed branches wherever they inclined to place themselves.

The figures were ghastly things, horrid creatures: Some seemed trusting, appealing, and kind, while others seemed suspicious, ugly, and rotten combined.

Though all were the same.

They breathed in heavy breaths as they did their noble deeds. Some licked their fingers, while others squeezed in their toes; yet, none seemed to become pleased. So they squealed in disproval.

One and another, while often most together, the Men-with-Sticks took their branches and flung them deep into the depths of the well, again and again; this eventually satisfied them all to an extent. When finished, for the time being, the things clapped their hands together and cavorted about with speeches that blatantly, and acceptably, voiced entitlement.

Again came the horde of floating fingers, which began to point themselves at the girl once more, adding laughs to complete the desired effect. This time however, the spectacle was paired with a flowing stream of red, one that fell from the nearby inflicted well.

How horrid it was.

Yet, somehow, Harlot found strength and continued on (which I will forever be made speechless by: the such can never be compared).

On and on the girl pressed herself, and then on to another place, which does not exist: She was met with the sight of a man trying to dig a hole in a river with a shovel; he attempted again and again, trying to find an opening, but he would never find one. Next she saw a man who had no limbs, only a stump; he could not move and would stay still, never to be able to extend any part of himself. Then she saw a horde of men searching for pockets upon a rock; they attempted the pressing of their fingers into the stone with all their might, but all they achieved were cracked bones and teeth that bit with a staggering firmness.

The sights Harlot witnessed were many, though never enough to achieve justice (if justice could ever be achieved: No).

With much effort, and a long searching, the girl managed to find the roots of the tree that she had been forced to fall below. She climbed them, making herself up and up and up.

Alas she made herself back to the trunk of the tree, but there were no red-dresses there.

So she made herself onto the top, where the leaves laid so high the below.

Harlot made a sound.

There was no answer.

CHAPTER IV

IN A FIELD FILLED WITH FLOWERS

And so, the girl made herself back towards her friends, back towards the trunk of the tree.

Without exchanging words, Harlot, Blue Spek, Pik-Pek and Lady made themselves outside the boundaries of the garden walls, eventually finding a place that does not exist: a liberated path covered in the colour of blue.

Indeed the way was ever so pleasant: The mouthfuls of trees that ringed around were blue, the glowing mushrooms that grew along were blue, and the round lights that leapt about were blue, which were all accompanied by the chiming and rhyming of flower-bells.

For a harmonious while, the beings continued on, until they met the sight of a flower field in the distance. Though famished, hollow cheeked, and thinned from her encounters, the girl became excited and animated by what she saw.

It was all so stimulating.

Harlot ran and ran and ran and ran and ran and ran, until finally, she joined a gathering of blossoming flowers of every colour and every kind, as well as that of blue. Oh how the girl felt as she made herself into the wondrous valley, pressing her fingertips onto the tops and the in-betweens of the splendid beings; it was a wonder filled feeling indeed, in which all enjoyed.

As Harlot continued forward with wanting steps, she joined the flowers in their blossomings, flourishing in happiness with all of those around her.

The girl looked towards her friends, and then towards the sky, one that had begun to drip with a joyous contemplation. The dripplets of wetness made themselves down towards, onto, into, and through her; she very much enjoyed the situation, sharing pleasure with all, pleased to be where she was.

Harlot was within a field of flowers.

End of Volume III

Upon a flower a word became
But soon it fell as was its name
The piper paid and played his game
And so have you though without the shame

** The prior presented was the first, second, and third volumes
of Harlot's encounters in the Land of Ick and Eck **

The End